SOULSAVER

SOULSAVER

JAMES STEVENS-ARCE

HARCOURT, INC.

NEW YORK   SAN DIEGO   LONDON

www.harcourt.com

A short-story version of *Soulsaver* appeared in the September 1983 issue of *Isaac Asimov's Science Fiction Magazine*, vol. 7, no. 9.

Library of Congress Cataloging-in-Publication Data
Stevens-Arce, James.
Soulsaver/James Stevens-Arce.—1st ed.
p.   cm.
ISBN 0-15-100472-2
I. Title.
PS3569.T454 S68 2000
813'.6—dc21   00-035056

Designed by G. B. D. Smith
Text set in Weiss
Printed in the United States of America
First edition
J I H G F E D C B A

With special love and gratitude to my wife, Tita, and our children Ian and Tara, as well as to my father, Jimmy, my mother, Estrella, and my brother Paul

I

"God bless us all, San Juan, and bless *you* for tuning in to W-G-O-D, where we praise the Lord twenty-four hours a day by playing all His heavenly hits without commercial interruption thanks to *your* generous donations! It is a beautiful May morning in the Greater San Juan Metroplex of the State of Puerto Rico in the Year of Our Lord 2099, and it's good, good, *good* to be alive! This next number goes out to all you highly holy Brothers and Sisters listening. Maybe *I* can't see you, but *He* knows who you are!"

My headband is tuned to San Juan's most righteous praised-be-Jesus music station. It rocks my soul, and I am Howie Happy.

"We're coming at you live with "Cristo Te Ama / Jesus Loves You," the latest Spanglish end-of-the-world hit by the hottest group in contemporary Christendom—the Make a Joyful Noise unto the Lord Gospel Maniacs! Hallelujah,

Brothers and Sisters! The hits just keep on coming on W-G-O-D! Why? Because *He* wants it that way!"

> *We will all fly to Heaven*
> *When that Glory Morning's done,*
> *We shall gather by the river*
> *At the setting of the sun,*
> *Our sweet Shepherdess shall call us*
> *To her bosom one by one,*
> *And dear Jesus will embrace us*
> *When the Second Coming comes.*

I feel Tommy Terrific. W-G-O-D is kicking off the hour with my favorite song, and the happy salsa-gospel beat sets my head to bobbing as I navigate the Corps FreezVan down a cobblestoned hill in Old San Juan past La Rogativa. Every schoolkiddy knows that the century-old group statue of a mitered bishop leading a parade of the faithful holding torches aloft commemorates the time five hundred years ago when Dutch invaders laid siege to the then-walled city. When the townspeople were on the verge of surrender from starvation, the bishop led a torchlight procession through the narrow streets imploring the Lord for a miracle. Next morning, the invaders were gone, leaving behind as the only traces of their presence burnt-out cookfires, mounds of garbage, and hundreds of the stinking trenches that served as their latrines.

The bishop called it a miracle. Centuries later, some unsaved revisionist historians tried to persuade folks that God had had nothing to do with it. Get this. They claimed that the invaders mistook the procession for the arrival of Spanish reinforcements, and lost the desire to continue their campaign, believing that the months they had spent laying siege to the city had been for nothing. These historians would have folks believe that that was the reason the Dutch decided to cut their losses and steal away in the night. But I say, so what if the invaders jumped to a bum conclusion? The people's prayers were answered. It just proves that God works in mysterious ways, ah?

Outside the van, the heat is sweltering. But inside, the cryopac support unit built into the roof keeps us cool as two corpsicles. My partner, Fabiola Muñoz, rides shotgun.

Fabiola is a good Christian woman. Face scrubbed, hair pulled back and tied off. No jewelry, except for a heavy gold ring with an abstract design that looks like two fish linked together. Like me, she wears a Suicide Prevention Corps of America standard issue red jumpsuit, a loose-fitting coverall that does not show a lot of the body beneath. But I know she has large breasts. A real Betty Boobs. Whenever a fit of smogcough hits her, they strain against her uniform.

The birthdate on her tag says 2/14/66, so she is thirty-three, eleven years older than me and a veteran officer. But she looks younger. I am just starting my novitiate. I have been with the Corps for barely a month.

Getting into the Corps is not easy. Soulsaving is a prestige position, and getting accepted, especially on your maiden try, is pretty special. The fact that I greased in my first time out makes me feel proud but humble, like maybe the Lord took a moment to smile down on this unworthy servant. But every time it hits me that my childhood dream has come true and that I am an honest-to-goodness soulsaver, my cup runneth over. Once I actually save my first soul, I will be positively floating.

Fabiola focuses on our dispatcher, Juanita Rosado, a fifty-something black Latina in a green SPCA jumpsuit who chatters away on the van's dashboard viddy screen. I can just make out her almost baritone voice through the music on my headband.

"Disciple One-Two, this is Prophet," Juanita says. "Self-inflicted death reported in the Santa Rosa Mall. Can you handle? Amen."

One-Two is Luis Zambrana's van. His partner, Nelly Rivera, answers: "This is Disciple One-Two, Prophet. We're on our way. ETA: two minutes, forty-two. Amen."

"Bless you, One-Two. Amen."

On the sidewalk ahead, a street preacher and his flock form a still pool in the river of humanity that streams endlessly through the narrow streets of the Old City. They wear headbands like mine, and, like me, they are rocking along with the Gospel Maniacs, quick-stepping in place to the bouncy conga-and-clave groove.

> *Hear me singing, Lord!*
> *Cristo te ama, aleluya,*
> *Cristo te ama*
> *Cristo te ama, aleluya,*
> *¡Aleluya!*

Civilians are so lucky. They get to wear those hip burnooses and brightly colored robes with bold Latino designs that cooled in when I was a kiddy. I love that style. It looks ultra Nicky Now, but still reminds us of the clothes that Jesus of Nazareth and the people of His time wore.

I sing along, not a care in the world. Out of the corner of my eye, I catch Fabiola looking at me dubiously, like she is thinking, Here is a kid who has got a lot to learn. Well, Sammy Sure I do, what does she expect? But maybe not as much as she might imagine, ah?

The viddy screen chimes, signaling that the next message is for our unit. "Disciple Five-Four, this is Prophet," Juanita Rosado says.

Fabiola gestures at my headband, but I am way ahead of her. I have already snuffed the volume, cutting the Gospel Maniacs off in mid-Cristo.

Juanita says, "Self-inflicted death at Caserío Madre Teresa, building six-two-two-niner. Can you handle? Amen."

Fabiola starts keying data into the dashboard brain before Juanita finishes. A grid map of the city wipes onto our screen. A pulsating line traces the fastest route to the Projects, while in a corner of the screen a chronometer inset flashes the estimated travel time for our unit.

"Disciple Five-Four acknowledging, Prophet. Can do. ETA is two minutes, thirty-one. Amen." Fabiola has this really professional-sounding voice, always calm and businesslike. I admire it. If only I could sound like that.

"Bless you, Five-Four," Juanita says. "Amen."

"Okay, Lorca, ¡vámonos!" Fabiola says.

I am way ahead of her. I am already triggering the eerie yodel that is the SPCA's trademark, and goosing the fuel input.

"Think you can find the place, Lorca?"

I wish she would call me Juan Bautista. But I am just a rookie on his first mission, and I guess she does not want me to forget it.

"Hey, I know Madre Teresa, Muñoz," I say.

That seems to shut her up. Maybe I am starting to earn a little respect.

We speed away, siren wailing.

In my rearview viddy screen, I can read the lips of the poor street preacher and his crowd straining to make themselves heard over our siren blast.

> *Cristo te ama, aleluya,*
> *¡Aleluya!*

2

So. Yet another SID at Madre Teresa, the super slum-clearance project to end all slum-clearance projects that the government built in 2096 and that now, only three years later, has itself turned into the Island's worst slum. They say it is Clive Claustrophobia among the poor, and I believe it. The rest of us are already living Sammy Sardine.

With the siren yowling, you can whip past in the special reserved lane on the elevado, skirting the vehicles poking along in the penance lanes, which is one of the reasons I like to pilot. I love our FreezVan with its sleek Chevyota lines and the SPCA logo on its sides—a white candle flame inside a sky-blue halo. The red letters encircling the upper half of the halo read: CUERPO ANTISUICIDA DE AMERICA; and the script around the lower half says the same in English.

In the end, of course, you always have to downramp to ground level and inch your way through the blessèd mob.

Crowds from the overly congested, mostly inoperative slidewalks spill out into the street, slowing us to a crawl.

Cristo, what a zoo.

Vandalized parks and rusting playgrounds. Graffitied buildings, walls, slidewalks, pavements.

Skin-and-bones beggars clamor for a handout: "¡Por favor, por favor, por favor!" Potbellied stickchildren totter about on spindly legs, their faces bony and hollow-eyed. Mommies with pregnant-again bellies lug babies in back slings, ignoring the kiddies' shrieks of hunger. Gaunt teeners lounge on each street corner, unemployed and looking for trouble. Wizened geezers play dominoes in the shade of rundown gazebos. Plump street preachers work the pockets of the skeletal faithful.

Everywhere, people, people, people.

Despite the van's air filters, the stench of weeks-old garbage seeps into the cockpit from mountains of uncollected trash bags. Even the welcome sign looks like folks have thrown turds at it.

BIENVENIDO AL CASERÍO MADRE TERESA

WELCOME TO THE MOTHER TERESA HOUSING PROJECTS

Skyhigh after skyhigh, the so-called vertical villages run row upon row in every direction as far as the eye can see. They would look like a field of giant grave markers, except that they are painted in shades of banana, avocado, orange, guava, and plum. They must have looked bright and cheerful when they were new, but now they are cracked and peeling.

So thick are the crowds in the street that I can barely keep the van moving forward. Fabiola says, "We're running late, rookie. Add dispersal overtones."

I add a piercing sonic to the siren's yodel. Folks grab their ears and wince in pain, but it is still exasperating how slowly they move aside. The more aggressive ones start pounding the vehicle's sides.

The situation is scary, but I swallow and try to sound like an old hand. "They sure don't like it, ah?"

"Anger is a sin," Fabiola observes dryly.

"Yeah," I say, grateful for the opening, "but it's hell to be hungry and Harvey Hopeless. There are so many of us and so blessèd little to go around." Fabiola says nothing. I figure this may be my chance to gain a little more respect, so I plunge ahead. "Still, you can forgive, but you can't justify sin, ah?"

Fabiola remains silent, but then I did not really expect her to answer. I take a deep breath. "Look at my mother," I say. "She was born in a caserío like this one, but she found a way out. Which proves faith will see you through. I mean, God tends to the needs of even the lilies of the field, ah?"

"You got it, rookie," Fabiola says in the same dry tone. "The Lord helps those."

We pull up in front of one of Madre Teresa's zillion identical skyhighs. The paint on this one is peeling worse than on its neighbors. I imagine that shade of raspberry trimmed in white looked cheerful and inviting when the residents first moved in.

The SID's apartment is small and crowded but clean. Two tiny bedrooms housing a family of sixteen, cheap plasteen baskets full of fresh wash on the dinette table. You know it is a big family just from how many different sizes of socks stick out of the washbaskets. They smell of cheap Washed in the Blood of the Lamb Biodegradable Laundry Detergent. Breakfast dishes still wet from rinsing sit by the kitchen window, drying in the breeze that flutters the curtains. A puff of wind blows the bathroom door ajar, exposing a chipped bathtub. The foot of a cocoaskinned woman hangs over the edge of the pink tub.

Though she has opened her veins from wrists to elbows—this self-inflicted meant business—the soulkiller is still warm. I dress the cuts, while Fabiola flips on her throat mike and starts her report. Fabiola is cool and professional. The me I want to be.

"Preliminary data. Carmen Colón. Female. Mulatto. Estimated age: thirty-six. Self-inflicted death, type two. Loading for delivery to Centro San Francisco de Asís."

The block priest and I confer in the hall. Father Tomás is a big-bellied cleric with an air of perpetual disapproval. "She waited until her husband left for his job at El Vertedero, packed the kids off to school, then sliced her wrists and bled to death in the tub," he mutters. He sounds Danny Disgusted, and I cannot say I blame him.

"Nancy Neat," I say.

"Fourteen children."

That explains his anger. Even if it *is* only a small family, what kind of woman leaves her kiddies in the lurch like this?

"Don't worry, Father," I tell him. "We'll bring their mami back."

Fabiola and I heft the skeletal body onto the air litter, and I whisk it out the door. Carmen Colón is light as a baby. Her papery skin looks ashen from loss of blood. Her mouth lolls open, and a string of spittle dribbles down her jaw. If SIDs only knew how ugly they look dead.

We are steering the meat through the crowd outside, Father Tomás bringing up the rear, when things turn ugly.

"Why don't you leave her dead, Bibletwister?" an angry voice hisses. "What kind of life is this to bring her back to?"

I cannot spot the speaker, but I know Double Jesus propaganda when I hear it. I get a little tense. Okay, maybe more than a little. But Fabiola and I follow standing orders, and ignore the heretic and the other mutterings and imprecations that follow. I guess maybe Father Tomás has other orders, because he gets furious and confronts the crowd.

"Who said that?" he shouts. "Who is the blasphemer?"

Like a hippo surrounded by storks, the fat priest bellies up to one stick-thin onlooker after another, glaring righteous accusation into each bony face. Their sunken eyes stare back, and always the voices come from behind him. While the crowd is distracted with the priest, Fabiola and I hurriedly load the air litter and its grisly cargo into the back of the van. We pull the hatch shut behind us and begin clipping sensors to the body from the cryopac overhead.

"Did you hear that?" I whisper to Fabiola. She remains silent. "*That* is New Christer talk," I say. "You can tell we're well into the Final Days!"

Fabiola does not look at me, focuses only on her work, the consummate professional under fire. "Let's just zip it and freeze this soulkiller, okay, rookie?" she says.

Cristo, I admire her!

Outside the van, Father Tomás has worked himself up into a lather. "God knows who you are, blasphemer!" he shrieks. "The One, True God sees all!"

"Ready here," Fabiola says. She glances up at me, expressionless. "How are you coming, Lorca?"

"Hookup complete, Muñoz." I hope I sound as cool and professional as she does.

"Check. Freeze her."

"Freezing SID."

I thumb the control pad in the van's side panel. A white haze envelops the body, and a deep hum fills the van. Eighteen seconds later, Carmen Colón is a corpsicle encased in white frost.

Ricky Routine, just like in training.

Outside, Father Tomás has not given up. "Beware, blasphemer!" he yells, loud enough for us to hear him through the van's thick insulation. "God will punish you!"

Fabiola mutters, "Amen," in that dry voice she likes to put on, and looks at me like she knows something I do not.

3

Siren howling, we shoot down the reserved lane of the Expreso Las Américas, racing against time. The twin rows of giant Caribbean coconut palms lining the median blur against the dirty blue sky. A corpsicle will keep barely half an hour in a van. If it is not at a center by then, you can kiss it good-bye.

The penance lanes in both directions look like huge vehicle storage compounds: hundreds of thousands of cars strung out nose to tail, going nowhere, hooting their Klaxons in rage or boredom. Mostly rustbuckets and rolling wrecks. Only high church folk can afford new wheels.

To our left, thick columns of black smoke and ash, each one wider across than four city blocks, roil up into the sky from El Vertedero to make their unending contribution to the smog. Designed as a landfill dump for the San Juan Metroplex in the late twentieth century, El Vertedero caught fire through spontaneous combustion almost a hundred years ago. When they discovered the fires were smoldering too deep beneath tons of trash to put out, the city fathers decided it would be cheaper to go on feeding the flames than to build a new dump. For almost a century now, the refuse of millions has flowed into El Vertedero and from there ascended into the heavens. When you drive by, the stink seeps in through even the most expensive filter system. And at night, the sky above glows a hideous orange. Poor folk frighten their kiddies into obedience by telling them El Vertedero houses las Puertas del Infierno—the Gates of Hell.

The Santurce skyline rises up ahead—slim modern sky-highs with rounded corners and curved edges mixed in with ugly, angular twentieth-century glass boxes. Fabiola codes data on our corpsicle into the onboard brain. On the viddy screen, Juanita Rosado chatters to other SPCA units. I am still thinking about that mob back at Madre Teresa. What is their problem, anyway?

I find I make better sense of things if I think out loud, especially if I am with somebody.

"Okay," I say to Fabiola, "I know some people resent the work we Corpsmen do, but our job is just another way of honoring God's laws. 'The life God makes only God may take'—that's the motto of the Suicide Prevention Corps of America, that's why people like you and me dedicate our lives to soulsaving."

Fabiola glances at me in disbelief. I guess she did not expect anything this deep from me. Well, maybe it is time she found out I can be full of surprises. This might be just the moment to get into a little of my philosophy of life.

"I believe in God and in His Instrument, the Shepherdess," I say, "and I believe the work I do is the Lord's work, and that in doing it I become like Jesus."

That sounds awfully good. Fabiola should be impressed with the kind of straight-and-narrow Christian she has drawn for a partner.

"My faith is strong and sturdy as a mighty oak," I conclude. "It's that simple."

A fit of coughing hits Fabiola. She slaps herself on the chest.

I look at her, wide-eyed. Is she having some sort of seizure? I am her partner. I have to help.

"What's wrong?" I say. I could kick myself for the quaver in my voice. "Should I do something? Should I stop the van? Do you need help? What should I do?"

A flutter of her hand. Is she losing consciousness?

No. She is...waving me away. Choking, she manages to say, "Smogcough." More coughing, thick with phlegm. That cannot be good. "Estoy...bien," she gasps out. She sucks in a deep breath, shudders.

"You don't sound too Tommy Terrific to me."

"I said I'm okay, Lorc—"

Another fit convulses Fabiola. With each cough, her breasts strain at her uniform like plump pigeons struggling in a sack.

I force my eyes to stay on the road. There is San Francisco up ahead. And not a moment too soon. Our corpsicle is coming up on the thirty-minute mark.

We careen through the gates of the resurrection center, whiz down the long, winding service drive between lush stands of bamboo and ferns, picking up speed. We are trailing another van by a hundred fifty meters, speeding maybe fifty meters ahead of a third, the wild shriek of our three sirens clashing in what I imagine must sound like a demonic chorus. The bamboo and ferns give way to handsome hibiscus hedges, their bright red amapola blossoms fat and sumptuous.

My attention ping-pongs between the road and the rise and fall of Fabiola's chest. My mouth is dry. I have trouble swallowing.

The loading dock comes into view up ahead, partially screened by a fall of violet bougainvillea. A sign at the end of the staging area reads:

CENTRO DE RESURRECCIÓN SAN FRANCISCO DE ASÍS
SALA PREPARATORIA

SAINT FRANCIS OF ASSISI RESURRECTION CENTER
PREPARATORY WARD

Luis Zambrana's van is already unloading. Cuso López's is pulling out. Rosario Fortuño's zips by behind us, plugs in two slots over. I hear the inhuman howl of more incoming sirens. So much fresh meat sends the dock into a feeding frenzy. As vans plug in, orderlies in powder-blue SPCA jumpsuits scramble. Running feet slap on the dock's rubberized flooring. Van hatches swing open, slam shut. Soulsavers shout commands. Orderlies rush about, hustling corpsicles out of each van and into the resurrection pipeline.

Papo Gómez, Luisa Plá, and Mayra Ruíz come pounding up to us. Papo springs open our rear hatch, while Luisa floats out the air litter and steers it away. Fabiola pops a tracer from the dashboard brain and presses it into Mayra's hand. Mayra chases after the litter, slips the tracer into its headrest, thumbs a datascreen to life.

The three orderlies rush the litter the rest of the way across the dock and vanish into the prep ward. From there, they will whisk Carmen Colón into the sala de resurrección, and the techs will run tests to see what needs to be restored. Scientists say there are no pain receptors in the brain, but everybody knows brain-cell regeneration hurts worse than death.

Fabiola slams the van's hatches shut, discovers me observing the hubbub.

"It's God's own miracle," I say.

"What?" Fabiola says.

"What we in the Corps do." I gesture at the SPCA logo on the side of our van. "Soon as she's prepped, they'll thaw her out, repair the damage, and resurrect her, good as new and ready to stand trial for trying to kill herself. Then, once she's atoned for her sin and been brought back into the Fold, she'll be sent home to her family. Susie Saved."

It is not likely the woman will try to kill herself again, either. For most folks, once through the ice is enough.

"So, okay, maybe I'm guilty of the sin of pride," I say, "but I feel Howie Happy knowing I helped save a soul. ¿Tú no?"

Fabiola gives me an odd look. "Me?" she says. "¡Oh, sí! Real Howie Happy."

4

The weather has gone to the Devil. Noontime temperatures soar into the low thirties, which is the high nineties to low hundreds in Fahrenheit. (Most of us are still getting used to the switch to metric.) August scorchers in early May, for Heaven's sake! The weather has changed everywhere over the past century, and Puerto Rico is no exception. Hotter summers, colder winters. The Atlantic has cooled two degrees from the melting of the ice caps. Weather mappers blame an effect named after some twentieth-century scientist called Greenhouse. Lucky for the local tourism industry that winter pilgrims ballooning down from the frozen Mainland still find the waters of the fifty-second state deliciously warm. We Islanders, though, are more sensitive to even small variations in temperature, so we do not hit the surf between October and March anymore. Too Freddie Frigid. Brr.

On a hot May day like today, though, a cold one is

more than welcome. I park by a stand on the Isla Verde beachfront tended by a skinny little vendor sweating in his blue-and-tan beach kaftan. The sign reads: PIRAGUAS/ SNO-CONES. Tart brown tamarindo syrup over shaved ice for Fabiola, sweet red frambuesa for me. I could put away a dozen of these raspberry delights.

Fabiola is a queer fish. She does not talk. She just stares out at the brilliant swells. My contacts darken to cut the glare. Cristo, it is a pretty day.

Farther down the coast, the ocean is brown from raw sewage and dumped chemicals. But this is a protected beach, reserved for tourists and local high church folk. Sure, keeping this stretch of shoreline clean and the water filtered of its usual sludge costs a bundle, but it is no more than God's best deserve. Along here, nature's colors shine almost too bright to be real—deep-blue water near the horizon, lime-green ocean just offshore, lacy whitecaps, golden sand, dark-green palm fronds.

The beach is thick with souls in bathing kaftans. They plunge through the breakers, laughing when the foamy wavetops flip them. Pilgrims on holiday sun their faces or join in group tai-chi exercises.

Fabiola and I suck at our piraguas and soak up the scene. A gust of wind whips off the ocean, stinging our hands and faces with grains of sand. The tang of sea salt cleans my lungs, and when I look straight up, I can barely make out the smog. It is good to be alive.

"¿Qué pasa?" I say. "What's tweaking you?"

Fabiola pretends not to hear, but I can be pretty difficult to ignore.

"You don't talk much," I say. "Anybody ever tell you that? You're a real Sally Shy."

Fabiola shifts her gaze from the horizon. Her eyes are the color of wet tea leaves, dark and self-contained. I wish I could look like that, but I do not know how.

"We've been partners for a month now," I say. "I'm just trying to be Floyd Friendly here."

"Kiddies today are all like that, aren't they?" she says.

"Kiddies today are all like what?" I say.

"You have no tact, no respect for privacy. No one is allowed to keep anything to herself."

This is the thanks I get for caring about how she feels? "Hey, you looked Trudy Troubled," I say. I shrug so she will know that it is no skin off my nose whether or not she wants to chat. "I thought maybe you might like to talk. I'm a good listener."

She snorts, shakes her head in disbelief. "When do you find the time? You never stop babbling in that silly kiddy slang of yours."

"Hey, if you don't want to talk about it . . ."

A few hundred meters offshore, a blimp glides by, its electroturbos humming. A silver whale swimming a thousand meters above the waves, it is headed for the nearby Luis Muñoz Marín International Aerodrome, carrying another load of sun seekers coming to the Caribbean for the weather Florida used to advertise.

"I don't want to talk to *you* about it." She turns back to the ocean.

Maybe I should be offended, but I let it slide. You need a thick skin to survive in this crowded world. And a sense of humor. I decide to forget Fabiola and just concentrate on the good things I am feeling. The raspberry syrup is thick and sweet, the shaved ice deliciously cold. I close my eyes and lose myself in the sensations. Hey, it is good to be alive, ah?

Fabiola's smogcough really mangles the moment.

5

My living cell in the unmarrieds' dorm is a prize, much bigger and nicer than the one I used to share with the Garófalo Brothers in our upper-school days. Its sprawling three-meters-by-two provides ample room for my cot, foldout desk unit, dresser and mirror, along with some shelves on which I display my raft of religious medals and sports trophies.

I was a pretty good volleyballer in upper school. Power hitter and center block. I have religious books, too, including *The Newer Testament*, as well as a conch shell larger than my head that I found the day of our senior class party at Luquillo Beach. The shell is rough and bumpy on the outside, but the inside is a sleek, shiny white shot through with a streak of magenta shading to dusty rose. There are still a few fine grains of sand inside, and you can smell the salty scent of the sea on it.

To break up the monotony of the gunite walls, I have put up styrofoil sculptures of the Last Supper, the Sacred Heart of Jesus, and the Assumption of the Virgin Mary. A wooden crucifix carved by hand in Mexico hangs directly above a hologram of the Shepherdess blessing the multitudes.

I really love this place, so when I get off duty and come in to change, it is rare that I do not have a song on my lips. Today it is that new Gospel Maniacs number.

> *For I know deep in my soul*
> *Our sweet Lord Jesus will return,*
> *He will cull the sheep out from the goats*
> *With Judgment fair and stern,*
> *He'll reward the pure and righteous*
> *With that joy for which they yearn,*
> *While those souls who chose for Satan*
> *Will forever after burn.*

While I sing, I peel off my jumpsuit, bobbing to the beat while avoiding my reflection in the mirror. I have never liked my face. It is too pretty, which I guess I owe to my mother. And I have this heavily muscled body, courtesy of my father. Folks say I have been blessed, and should not complain. And they are right. God has been good to me. But I cannot help wishing I looked a little more like the average chico, you know?

I clip the jumpsuit inside the cleaner, set the ultrasonics for Summer Weight, and slip into a stylish green robe with

Taíno Indian designs hand-painted in thick, primitive-looking brush strokes. I love civvies. They are real Kimmy Comfy.

The place of honor in my room belongs to my mother, Amparo. I have a full motion color hologram of her on my dresser, recorded when she was seventeen, a beauty with straight black hair and lime-green eyes, same as mine. In the holo, she blows a kiss, smiles a ravishing smile, and waves. Blows a kiss, smiles, and waves. Over and over, endlessly, per saecula saeculorum. The scene never changes, but I never tire of watching it.

As I head out the door, my mother blows me a kiss, smiles, and waves, blows me a kiss, smiles, and waves, like always. And, like always, I blow her a kiss and say, "God bless you, Mom!"

I know it is Sally Silly, but I feel maybe that makes her smile up in Heaven, too.

6

The rec room is at least ten times bigger than my room, with a giant wall screen, bank upon bank of snack dispensers, and a row of hot new holo games. We are talking *space.* I spot Eddie, Bebo, and Wilfredo Garófalo, who test games for Nippon Christian Electronics, across the room playing, respectively, *Demon Attack, Satan's Lair,* and *God's Hooks.*

On the wall screen, a muscular giant with shoulder-length blond hair squares off against a brawny, toad-faced thug. The thug must be beating the Hell out of the giant, because the color man, Brother Thaddeus "Headlock" McGillicuddy, sounds desperate.

"—and oh, my Lord," Brother Headlock cries, "the Lamb of God is in terrible trouble! The Devil Worshiper keeps body-slamming the sweet bejesus out of him and it looks like nothing this side of a miracle can save him now!"

I see her, and stop breathing.

She sits in profile, watching the viddy screen, eyes sparkling, face flushed, excited by the action in the ring. She looks my age, maybe a year older, with black hair and no makeup. She catches me staring and turns questioningly. She looks like my mother. Even her eyes are the same shade of green.

Suddenly the Lamb of God and the Devil Worshiper vanish, and there is the white-haired, craggy face of America's most belovèd viddy newsbreaker, Father Luther Martínez, looking like the wise old uncle we all wish we had. Delivered in his warm baritone, good news sounds marvelous, and bad news bearable.

"We interrupt *Hallelujah Wrestling* for this special news report direct from the District of Christ," Father Luther says. "Brothers and Sisters: the Shepherdess."

A darkened staircase curves up to a platform where a woman in flowing robes stands in stark silhouette, arms thrown wide to embrace the world. White mist breaks up her backlight into rays that flicker and flash like heavenly radiance from around her head and hands and arms and legs, and make her robe transparent enough to confirm that when the Lord was handing out fine bodies, she was standing at the head of the line.

An invisible choir sings the Shepherdess's signature tune.

> *I heard the voice of Jesus say,*
> *"Come unto me and rest."*

The lowest step blazes with an inner light, then the one above it, then the one above *it*. As the music swells, step after step blazes to life, one after the other, creating a magical wave of light that sweeps majestically upward toward the Shepherdess.

> "Lay down, thou weary one,
> Weary one, lay down."

The camera pursues the wave of light up the stairs, until the top step incandesces, *flash!*, and the Shepherdess's platform itself finally blazes into life. As the camera tracks in tighter and tighter on the Shepherdess's silhouetted face, the music builds—

> "Lay thy head on my breast!"

—and suddenly cuts off.

A pink beam lights the Shepherdess's face. The faithful gathered in the rec room gasp. No matter how many times you see her, the Shepherdess remains the most charismatic person alive. Not only was she a breathtaking beauty with a commanding presence in her twenties—I have seen the viddies over and over—but she has only grown in power and deepened in loveliness in her forties. Her smile dazzles. And when she speaks, her voice throbs with a deep joy and promise that stir me.

"Bless you, my Children," the Shepherdess says huskily.

"Bless you, dear Mother," we chorus back.

"I come to you today, Brothers and Sisters in Jesus, because the Lord last night sent me a vision—a vision of unholy evil loosed upon the world like a great black beast uncaged." The Shepherdess's eyes narrow. "I have seen the shadow of the Dark One spread across the land, and I have seen all that we hold pure and holy trampled and laid waste beneath his cloven hooves."

My dorm mates moan and murmur, "Sweet Jesus, no! Oh, sweet Jesus, no!"

"Sweet Jesus, yes," the Shepherdess says dolefully. "I have seen it." She looks sad. Then she brightens, her face and smile as warm as the sun. "But it need not come to pass," she whispers. "We can stop it. You and I and all our brethren who have surrendered themselves to the Lord, body and soul." She opens her arms to us. "*We* . . . can stop it from happening!"

"Instruct us, dear Mother!" the murmurers plead. "Tell us how!"

"More than ever before," the Shepherdess says, "we must beware of the Antichrists and their Godless lies."

Her eyes turn cold and unforgiving.

"We must search out the Judases among us, for they seek to destroy us."

My dorm mates glance around suspiciously, as though they might actually unmask a traitor plotting his schemes right here in the rec room. Cristo, what overly scrupulous consciences. Every well-fed one of us here *has* to be a good Christian. Otherwise, we would not *be* here. Only the children of priests and ministers and other important church folk get to live in the luxury dorms.

"Even as I speak," the Shepherdess whispers, "the followers of the so-called Twin Messiahs are plotting. Even as I speak, they conspire to destroy the Kingdom of Heaven on Earth, our holy Christian American nation."

The look of unutterable sadness on her face makes me long to comfort her, but instantly her eyes blaze with righteous determination. My heart leaps with joy.

"And so," she says, "in order to preserve our one great nation under God, in order to crush this terrible threat to God's Rule before it can do further—and perhaps irreparable—harm, the Bill of Rights is hereby temporarily suspended, in the name of Christ Jesus. Amen."

"Amen," we chorus.

"Bless you, my Children."

"Bless you, dear Mother."

The sweet face of the Shepherdess sublimates into a night view of the White House. A huge illuminated cross rises slowly from the front lawn.

"That concludes this special transmission from Washington, District of Christ," says Father Luther, materializing onscreen. We already feel exalted by the Shepherdess's quick, sure moves to stifle this cunning evil in its crib. Now, Father Luther's reassuring presence underlines the fact that good will surely wipe the floor with evil yet again, and all will be well.

"As you heard," Father Luther says, nodding thoughtfuly, "the Shepherdess has officially unmasked the so-called Twin Messiahs to reveal that, as many already suspected, they are the Antichrists of the Final Days. She also suspended the Bill of Rights. We now rejoin our regularly scheduled program, already in progress."

The wrestling match reclaims the screen. Fortunes have flip-flopped, and the Lamb of God has the upper hand. He is mopping up the ring with the Devil Worshiper. Brother Headlock is on the verge of apoplexy. "—and good Lord, Brothers and Sisters," the monk practically shrieks into his microphone, "a miracle has occurred and the Lamb of God has turned into a veritable lion!"

The Lamb does seem to have received a lion-sized dose of Grace. He strains with every ounce of strength, jerks the Devil Worshiper high over his head, swings him upside down so his ugly toad mug is mashed against the Lamb's hard ridged stomach and his hairless toad legs kick frantically in the air in front of the Lamb's angelic face. Now that he has got the short end, the Devil Worshiper begs for mercy. Typical.

To err is human, to forgive divine. We all know that. But the Lamb also knows the kind of two-faced, Bible-mocking heathen he is dealing with. The Lamb sucks wind, and digs deep inside himself for the strength to hoist up the Devil Worshiper a little nearer, my God, to Thee. Then, he smashes the errant sinner headfirst into the canvas. The Devil Worshiper shrieks and flops about like a wounded manatee. And the Lamb—*whap!*—drops on top of him and—*zap!*—pins him. One! Two! Three! The good guys win!

Brother Headlock is beside himself. "Witness to this, Brothers and Sisters!" he cries. "The Lamb of God, a man who was on the very *brink* of perdition, has found the strength in his soul to say the Devil nay and carry the day in the Lord's Sweet Name! Bless him, Brothers and Sisters, bless him!"

I punch my fist into the air and cry out, "Bless him!" just

as the girl with my mother's eyes does, too. We look at each other and laugh. She lowers her gaze, and brushes past me, murmuring, "Excuse me, Brother." At the door, she hesitates, glances back over her shoulder and flashes me a look full of the same promise that stirred me when I heard the voice of the Shepherdess. Then she is gone.

No other girl has ever looked at me quite like that. I wish I could follow.

On the viddy screen, Brother Headlock grins at us, his freckles aglow with anticipation.

"Coming up next, Brothers and Sisters," he says, "a ladies tag-team event you will not want to miss—a steel-cage grudge match between the Little Sisters of Mercy and the Whores of Babylon."

7

"How can I be of help, my son?"

"Forgive me, Father, for I have sinned."

Father René speaks from the monitor screen of a confession booth in my dorm chapel. My face peers out from his screen in a confessor's booth located in the bowels of the Northern Sector Penance Command Center near Aguas Buenas. Jokesters call it Sin Control.

Father René has been my confessor since I made my First Communion at the age of seven. I have never met him in the flesh, but he looks like he may be in his early forties. His face is heavily pockmarked. I presume that the pocks are the scars of adolescent acne—something I have never had to worry about, thanks be—and that he has chosen not to have the blemishes repaired as a mortification of the flesh. His gentle, understanding manner does not seem to mesh with his streetwise looks. He is the only priest I know who is not fat.

Father René touches his index finger to his lips. He is not shushing me. He has just gone into what he calls his pensive mode and is ready to listen.

"What is the nature of your transgressions, Juan Bautista?" he says.

"Carnal, Father."

I try to sound dispassionate. It is not easy.

"Describe them to me."

I take a deep breath. "I work with an older woman, and when I'm alone, I find myself thinking about her. A lot."

"What is her name?"

"Fabiola Muñoz."

"And what kind of thoughts do you entertain about this Fabiola Muñoz, my son?"

"I . . . spend hours picturing her breasts, her belly, her thighs." My nose itches. I rub it with the side of my finger. "Real Cherry Cheesecake stuff, you know?"

"I understand."

"And there's a new girl about my age in the unmarrieds' dorm who has a way of looking at me that . . . stirs me up. She has green eyes." As though that explains everything.

"And what is her name?"

"I don't know. The problem is, I know it's not proper just to go up and start talking to her, but I don't know anyone who could introduce us. Dwight Dilemma, huh?"

"How old are you now, Juan Bautista?"

"Twenty-two."

"Then there is no sin. This is your wedding year, and does not the law say to multiply and fill the earth? Your thoughts are as they should be. Unless...is the older woman wed?"

"Fabiola is a widow. And lonely, I think."

"Then it is permitted to lust in your heart." Father René smiles encouragingly. "Have you sinned otherwise, Juan Bautista?"

"No, Father."

"Then there is nothing to forgive." He traces the Sign of the Cross in the air. "Go in peace."

"Praise the Lord."

"Praise Him."

The Digital Jesus appears on my monitor. "G-G-G-Go and sin no m-m-more, my son." The programmed stutter is meant to make Him seem more human, but I find it annoying.

Transmission bands between confessionals are supposed to be leakproof, but a murmur on my speaker makes me press my ear to the grill. I make out Father René saying, "Yes, my child?" To eavesdrop on another's Confession is a sin, because it infringes upon the privacy of the sacrament, but I listen anyway. I am sure I recognize the answering voice.

The girl with my mother's eyes.

She says, "Forgive me, Father, for I have sinned."

Wo!

Just like me.

8

"¡Dios mío!" the apartment complex supervisor says, "I have been managing buildings for forty-three years, and nothing like this ever happened to me before."

The supervisor of the San Ciriaco Apartments is a skinny geezer named Sacrovir Sosa. Fabiola and I are up on the building's lowest ledge with him, looking at a dead man's body. It is sprawled facedown on the scorching concrete, one arm dangling over the ledge. The arm is as white as chalk.

"He lived on the thirty-fifth floor," Sosa says.

This SID has burst open like a ripe melon—guts, skull, brains shattered and smeared all over. I feel sick.

Dozens of shiny black crows eye us from their perches on the colonial Spanish-style wrought-iron lampposts that frame the building entrance and the leafy branches of the húcares that line the street. They hope we will leave them something to snack on. The cuervos had best be careful that they themselves do not become meals for the hungry and homeless of this neighborhood.

"June is for jumpers," Fabiola mutters.

By scattering his brains over ten square meters of ledge, the soulkiller has made it impossible for the médicos to bring him back. Mickey Mess. Why do people do this to themselves?

"His wife died two weeks ago," Sosa says. Some people volunteer information to be helpful, some to puff themselves up by appearing to be in the know. I have not figured out which type Sosa is yet. "Smog cancer," Sosa says. "He was crippled from the hips down, and she took care of him."

"Okay, Juan Bautista," Fabiola says, "let's get to it. Scoop up all visible tissue and freeze it."

It seems like a complete waste of time to me.

"What's the point?" I say. "You can't put Humpty Dumpty back together again. This soul is zooming straight to Hell, no second chance. Davey Damned."

Fabiola gives me a hard look. "The regs say freeze the meat and haul it in," she says. "It's not your job to decide if the soulkiller beats the system."

I look at the bloodless body lying on concrete hot enough to scorch dead flesh. "I didn't know you *could* beat the system."

Inside the Chevyota, the air is blessedly cool, and I come back to life. I try to move as briskly as Fabiola, hooking up the cryopac sensors to the body with what I hope is similar silent efficiency.

When the SID is prepped, Fabiola says, "Ice him."

I thumb the freeze control. The guy's skin is as white as the haze that envelops him. The deep hum of the cryopac relaxes me a little.

"Why do you suppose they kill themselves?" I say. I have to admit, I am feeling kind of Danny Depressed.

Fabiola regards me coldly, maybe even with a little disdain. "Now, why would a righteous muchacho like you ask a question like that, Juan Bautista?"

Such hostility! It leaves me speechless. What have I done to deserve this?

With a challenging look, she holds my stunned gaze. "Meat's frozen," she says. "Let's haul it."

Just as though nothing has happened.

9

We race for San Francisco de Asís.

Siren wailing, Fabiola and I whiz down the empty reserved lane. Motionless noon-hour traffic clogs the penance
lanes. No trace of a breeze outside. The palm trees lining
the median look painted against the sky.

"Do you live alone?" I say.

Fabiola gives me a weird look. "Why do you ask?"

"Just making conversation."

Up ahead lies the interchange that links the De Diego
and Las Américas Expressways. I swing from the reserved
lane onto the general access ramp and cut between two
sluggish hovertrucks headed for Arecibo and Mayagüez
with cargoes of vacuum-dried food. The big one is carrying
tuna, the other processed seaweed. I like tuna, but raw.
Anytime I have a little extra, I treat myself to a visit to El
Paraíso de Sushi Número Tres. Sure, it can mangle your

credit if you are not careful. But, hey, we pass this way but once, ah?

I switch channels on the dashboard viddy screen, and replace Juanita Rosado with a CACNN newsbreaker. While we are hauling meat in, we are officially out of the loop. But even if we were on available status, any call from Juanita would automatically override anything else we might punch up.

"Despite government emergency efforts," the news-breaker says, "the plague of locusts that descended on Argentina just two days ago has wiped out that embattled country's wheat crop.

"Speaking in his capacity as President of All the Russias, His Eminence the archbishop of Moscow announced today the voluntary reintegration of Finland into the Motherland.

"And, in special session late last night, a motion to grant the lunar villes independent nation status was vetoed in the Reunited Nations Security Council.

"This is Kevin Lesotho, Christian American Capsule News Network."

"If you live alone," I say, "I was thinking you might like to get married again."

Fabiola turns toward me slowly. "To *you?*"

"It's my wedding year," I say. She looks surprised. "Didn't you know?"

I start ticking points off on my fingers. "I'd make a good husband. I keep the Commandments. I'm a God-fearing Christian. And I have other virtues."

"Why me?"

"You're the only woman I know well enough."

"My," she says, "you certainly know how to sweep a girl off her feet." She coughs raggedly. "Look, we've worked together all of two months. You don't know a blessèd thing about me."

"I know what I need to know. I admire your professionalism and self-confidence. I want to be like you."

"No, you don't."

"¿Por qué no?"

"Because you would be a very unhappy young man."

As I flick the Chevyota into reverse, she says, "Let's try to plug into the dock a little more gently this time, shall we?"

Betty Bitch.

I∅

Back on the elevado, traffic in the penance lanes is up to barely ten klicks per hour, while we cruise along the reserved lane at more than a hundred kph. The palm trees lining the median droop in the heat. Their fronds hang listlessly. They remind me of those people you see on the street who you know have finally given up. I have my headband tuned to W-G-O-D, listening to the Gospel Maniacs.

> *Why don't you swing down, chariot,*
> *Stop and let me ride?*
> *Swing down, chariot,*
> *Stop and let me ride?*

I am bobbing my head in time to the syncopated cumbia beat, moving my lips as I sing along silently. I should be nursing hurt feelings, but instead I feel good, good, *good*.

Rock me, Lord,
Rock me, Lord,
Calm and easy

Fabiola rides shotgun, eyeing the passing landscape impassively. She looks . . . what? The word "morose" leaps to mind. I heard it last Sunday on that new educational viddy game show *In the Beginning Was the Word*. It was the "Word of the Day," and it sure seems to fit Fabiola now. Miss Molly Morose.

I got a home on the other side.
Why don't you swing down, chariot,
Stop and let me—

The viddy screen chimes and the words TOP PRIORITY BULLETIN replace Juanita Rosado onscreen. Fabiola nudges me, but I am a lot more alert than she gives me credit for. I am already snuffing the volume on my headband.

Father Luther Martínez appears, eyes twinkling reassuringly. "We interrupt our regular programming," he says, "to bring you this special, personal message from our belovèd Shepherdess."

The Shepherdess addressing the nation again so soon? Must be something *big*. Still, Father Luther did not look especially concerned.

The White House Choir slips into *I Heard the Voice of Jesus* as the Shepherdess appears "live from the Rose Garden" surrounded by red and white blooms. The choir continues, humming the melody behind her now. The

Shepherdess's seductive voice floats above their sweet choral sound.

"Bless you, my Children," the Shepherdess says.

"Bless you, dear Mother," Fabiola and I answer automatically.

Today, the Shepherdess does not bother with a lead-in. She is primed and ready, and jumps in with both feet, preaching hot and heavy from the first word out of her mouth.

"I spoke with the Lord last night, Children!" the Shepherdess cries.

In the background, her choir choruses, "Praise Him!"

"I prayed long and hard for guidance!"

"Guidance, Lord!"

The Shepherdess lifts both arms, palms facing us defensively. "For Satan is loose in the land," she whispers, as though fearful the wrong person may overhear, "pretending to be the second incarnation of Our Lord Jesus Christ!"

"Deliver us, Lord!"

The Shepherdess holds her arms out to her sides. "And I said, 'Lord, tell me what we should do, because this is one tough call.'"

"Tell us, Lord!"

The Shepherdess's hands come together, palm against palm, as though in prayer. "And the Lord spoke to me, Children," she says in a voice mingling awe and joy. "The Lord spoke to me, saying, 'Daughter, do you want to set the brakes to Satan and his evil minions? Do you want to bring the rise of the false prophets to a screeching halt? Do you want to just plain *stop* the Antichrists dead in their evil tracks?'"

"You know it, Lord!" the choir choruses.

The Shepherdess nods slowly. "That is exactly what I said. 'You know it, Lord.' And the Lord, He spoke to me again, saying, 'Then, Alma Lucille, you must outlaw the New Christer Cult, and there is just no two ways about it!'"

"Praise Him!" cries the choir. "Praise Him! Praise Him!"

The Shepherdess stalks grimly toward us from among the roses. Her footsteps ring out on the flagstones. Suddenly she stops, looking directly through the camera into our eyes.

"And so today, as of twelve noon Eastern Prayerlight Time," the Shepherdess says grimly, "the so-called New Christer Cult has been declared a tool of the Adversary and officially outlawed, in the name of Our Lord. Amen."

The choir bursts into Handel's *Hallelujah Chorus*.

"Your minister or confessor can answer any questions," the Shepherdess says. "Bless you, my Children."

"Bless you, dear Mother," I say automatically.

Fabiola stares sightlessly at the peaks of the Cordillera Central in the distance. They are a dark smudge through the smog, even on a sunny day like today. You can hardly make out El Yunque to the east, the anvil-shaped mountain where the last remnants of America's only rainforest struggle to survive. Fabiola's eyes are red-rimmed. Her face looks old.

"The Lord should have spoken a long time ago," I say. I whistle a snatch of *The Hallelujah Chorus*. "So, is that a no, then?" I ask.

"What?" Fabiola says.

The woman is a million miles away. What is her problem?

"About getting married?" I say.

She stares at me. Maybe she wants to play hard to get.

"Let me think about it," she says distantly.

Even her features seem blurred, like the cloud-covered silhouette of El Yunque in the distance.

"Okay," I say, "but don't dawdle, ah?"

I am raring to fulfill my Christian duty.

II

I am in church when it finally happens.

Morning light streams in through brightly colored stained glass windows depicting the Stations of the Cross, only these renditions are decorated with tropical motifs— coconut palm trees, rainforest ferns, tree frogs, colorful Puerto Rican parrots. Mother Arantxa speaks the Mass in traditional Latin, facing the congregation. Angela serves as deaconess. When Mother Arantxa raises the Host, Angela rings the bells.

Angela is the name of the girl with the green eyes. Angela Amador. I found out she is an acolyte of the Daughters of Mary and works in the Bureau of Indulgences.

The priestess intones, "Sanctus, sanctus, sanctus," then consumes the Host. Angela sneaks a glance at the pews. I catch the movement of her head out of the corner of my eye. My own head is modestly bowed, but I get the idea she is looking for me. It stirs up a funny feeling in my belly. The priestess extends the chalice to Angela. She pours in wine and water from separate cruets. The priestess murmurs the words of Consecration over the chalice, then makes the Sign of the Cross.

"In nomine Patri, et Filii, et Spiriti Sancti."

I bless myself, whispering the words along with the priestess as she raises the chalice. Angela rings the bells.

"Sanctus, sanctus, sanctus."

The priestess drinks the wine. Angela glances my way again. I keep my head bowed.

The people around me rise for Communion, and shuffle toward the front of the church down the center aisle. I go with them. Eyes modestly downcast, we line the altar rail. As deaconess, Angela is in charge of placing the Communion bread on the tip of each person's tongue. When she approaches, we each present ourselves in the same way: eyes closed, lips parted, tongue slightly extended.

But when she slips the wafer into my mouth, her finger traces my lips and touches my tongue. *Zing!* Like a spark leaping from her skin to mine.

The tip of her finger tastes salty, like raw sea-urchin eggs.

I look boldly into those eyes so like my mother's. That quick glance away and back—does she remember me? Yes! Is that trace of a smile on her lips meant for me alone? And the really important question: Did she touch me on purpose?

My mind swirls with wonderings and questions, with speculations and possibilities. Whatever the facts, it is a new ball game. Now that she has ministered to my spirit, I am finally free to speak to her.

After services, I wait for her outside the sacristy. The usual Sunday multitudes mill past. I get jostled and bumped repeatedly, but I do not mind. I do not even mind the oppressive noonday heat, or the sweat beading up on my brow and under my arms and starting to slither down my breastbone and spine.

Angela takes longer than I had expected. I alternate between standing impatiently in one place like a boulder that parts a rushing torrent and nervously fighting my way through the crowd from one end of the walkway to the other.

It would be a beautiful morning if the smog was not thicker and browner than usual today. I cast frequent glances at the sacristy door, eager for it to open, but for the longest time it remains stubbornly shut.

Then it swings wide. My spirits soar.

But it is only the priestess. I greet her dutifully. "Bless me, Mother."

Mother Arantxa tosses back a "Bless you, Child," without even looking at me. She bustles by and vanishes into the crowd.

I glare at the door. It remains closed, shut, sealed, cerrada. I furrow my brow, and will it to open. ¡Milagro! It does! And, at long last it is Angela, breathtaking in a burgundy robe. Is her appearance as if on cue meant as some sort of sign?

She approaches me casually, wending her way through the passing multitudes. She does not seem at all surprised to see me. The closer she gets, the clearer it becomes that she is almost as tall as I am. I had not noticed this before. I am curious about the shape of that long body beneath the loose cloth.

I wade through the river of faithful going about their Sunday errands, and meet her halfway. "Bless you, Sister," I say.

She casts her eyes down modestly, and smiles with a sweet shyness. "Bless you, Brother." Her smile knocks the breath out of me.

A huge pause. "Hey, my name is Juan Bautista." I kick myself mentally. Can I think of nothing more original to say?

"Hey," she says, "I know."

Her soft voice and modestly downcast eyes put me in mind of Our Lady. But there is an underlying boldness about Angela that I have never noticed in any other woman, not even in Fabiola. I feel real Willie Wetdream, like when I lie in bed in my room and picture Fabiola's thighs.

"What do you mean, you know?" I ask.

"You're a Corpsman," Angela says. "I've seen you in your jumpsuit. You look Buddy Beautiful in your uniform, like an angel of mercy." She cocks her head to one side, gives me a mischievous smile. "Don't *you* know *my* name?"

I melt, but I do not want her to see that she has such a

powerful effect on me, at least not yet. I laugh and clear my throat. "Sure," I say in as casual a voice as I can muster. "Angela Amador."

Her smile grows into a grin. "Do you know I work in the Bureau of Indulgences?" She waltzes around me, giving me the once-over in a teasing way. "If you've got a sin to atone for and enough credit, I sell you the proper indulgence and, *zap!*, you're Peter Pure again."

"Kind of like Mary Magdalene in reverse," I say.

"How do you mean?"

"You make people feel good by *cleansing* them of sin."

Angela's reaction combines surprise and delight. "I never thought of it that way before." She looks at me with new interest. "Do you want to go for sushi?"

Now it is my turn to look at her with surprise and delight. "You like sushi?" I say excitedly. A kindred soul?

She nods enthusiastically. "I *love* sushi," she says, as though sharing a special secret with me. "Little white rice balls crowned with thick slices of delicious raw tuna, yellowtail, grouper, shrimp, and chewy octopus, all dipped in special shoyu sauce?" She shivers with pleasure. "Just thinking about it makes my mouth water!"

"Me too!"

For a moment, she looks at me with a thoughtful expression, like she is trying to read something in my eyes, like she is trying to make up her mind about something. Then she smiles again.

"There's a great place nearby," she says, suddenly shy again. "El Paraíso de Sushi Número Tres. Do you know it?"

My heart leaps. *"Know* it? I *love* El Paraíso de Sushi Número Tres."

We set off for the restaurant, walking comfortably side by side. Even as we are swept along by the endless stream of humanity, I feel like we are alone together.

I look at Angela, and she at me, and neither of us sees anyone else.

"You love sushi and you've got green eyes just like my mother had," I say. "Maybe I should marry you."

Angela laughs. "Maybe you should."

I like the way she laughs.

12

Sunday duty pays double. I am thinking ahead to Monday when I plan to apply that extra credit to another sushi feast. Fabiola and I have just dropped off a load of meat at San Francisco when I remember that Monday is the Fourth and I will have to drive the van in the Corps' section of the Independence Day parade. Well, okay, dinner then instead of lunch.

It has been an evil Sabbath—half a dozen self-inflicteds in less than four hours. Six would-be soulkillers saved, if you look on the bright side.

A CACNN newsbreaker, one of the Asians, I forget his name, reports on the dashboard viddy screen:

"A delegation of Cuban prelates arrived in civil war–torn Mexico today to begin a long-awaited mission of peace, and started by calling for a halt to atrocities on both sides.

"Two controversial new viddy bios scheduled to go online opposite each other tonight will slug it out toe to toe as both claim to present a modern perspective on the recently canonized twentieth-century religious figure now known as Saint Elvis.

"And lineups will be announced later today for Tuesday night's hundred seventieth National and American League All-Star Game scheduled for Yomiuri Stadium in Osaka, Japan.

"This is Nguyen van Tranh, Christian American Capsule News Network."

It is a gray, drizzly Sunday, the kind that can get your spirits down even if you are not pulling extra duty. The palm trees along the median look hunched over and depressed. Fabiola stares out the passenger window. Molly Morose. It is certainly the right day for feeling that way. Looks like it is up to me to perk things up.

"Maybe it's my imagination," I say, "but I think more suicides are popping off."

Fabiola glances over at me, then looks back out at the rain with no change in her hangdog expression. I have seen how that kind of attitude can be contagious, so I am not going to let her negativism infect me.

"Don't people understand that God makes so many of us because He loves us so much?" I say.

Fabiola says nothing. I guess she is still in her you-talk-too-much-rookie mode. But I do not care. If I had wanted to work under a vow of silence, I would have signed up with the Teamster Trappists. Besides, I have a valid point to make.

"It doesn't take a genius to get that," I say. "It's all there in the Catecismo."

She acts like she is in a trance, staring out the window at the passing scenery, hardly blinking. I raise my voice a little, determined to get through to her.

"Can't they see that the overcrowding and the harsh living conditions are a test of our love for Him," I continue, "and that the reward in Heaven will be all the sweeter for our having borne the sufferings of this vale of tears without complaint?"

We are headed west on usually crowded Boca de Cangrejos Road. Playa de Aviones, Airplane Beach, is on our right. Ordinarily, this huge public balneario would be carpeted with maybe half a million Sunday beachgoers, but the constant rain has kept them home and washed the shoreline clean, staining the normally golden sand light brown. Dirty gray-green breakers crash the length of this unprotected beach. The angry water looks cold and forbidding. Beyond the reef line, where the deepening ocean begins to shade from brown to blue, a few hardy souls race one- and two-person baby catamarans across the sludgy swells. With their bright rainbow sails, the boats look like butterflies skimming across a mud hole.

To our left, flocks of silvery commercial dirigibles are in the process of detaching from or hooking up to their moorings at busy Luis Muñoz Marín International Aerodrome. Departing flights hum by over us as they begin to fan out toward the gray horizon. I wonder why folks have not started calling this stretch of coastline Blimp Beach. Fuel-devouring commercial jetliners were pretty much phased out before I was born, but I guess old habits die hard.

The viddy screen chimes, startling Fabiola back from the ranks of the living dead.

Thank God, I think, something to break the monotony. But immediately I feel bad. The call signal can only mean that one more despairing soul has traded the road to Salvation for the expressway to Hell.

"Disciple Five-Four, we've got a reported SID at the Bayamón bullet-train station," Juanita Rosado says. "Can you take it? Amen."

"Can do, Prophet," Fabiola says, her voice crisp and professional. "ETA is two minutes twelve. Amen."

"Bless you, Five-Four. Amen."

I light the siren, and prepare to swing the van across the median by cutting over the access lane we are approaching.

Another lost soul to save. Edie Excitement!

I cannot help feeling good.

13

Our seventh self-inflicted today is a tiny, birdlike woman.

We barrel into the guiderail area, siren yodeling. The crowd from the boarding platform mills about one of the support pylons. The station manager limps over.

"It was horrible," she mutters, keeping her voice low to prevent the rubbernecks from overhearing. "She must have stepped out in front of it. You'd be surprised how many people try to take this way out. They think it'll be quick, painless, and permanent. Although maybe you wouldn't be surprised. Anyway, there's nothing anyone can do when that happens. The Mayagüez Express whizzes through here at just under five hundred klicks per hour. And that particular gravlev doesn't stop here."

The victim just shredded herself. Her head rolled free in one piece, but the body looks like it has been through a thresher.

The tiny head lies on a bed of gravel. Its hair is cropped short. A gold crucifix dangles from one ear. One eye is closed, so it looks like she is winking. The open eye is the color of wet tea leaves.

"Ghoulish, isn't it?" the manager says.

"¡Dios mío!" I whisper. What a terrible way to die.

Fabiola's face is ashen. Her eyes look sick. Why, I do not know. She has always been Our Lady of the Iron Stomach. But she handles the situation like a pro. We gather up the scattered meat, freeze the pieces, and turn them in at San Francisco. All Ricky Routine.

As we hum away from the center, Fabiola is still white as a Communion wafer. I am ticked off.

"Another sinner who's slithered into Satan's embrace," I say. "Danny Depressing."

Fabiola just broods. I hate that.

"Sometimes I wonder why we bother," I say. "Let them die and good riddance, ah? But then I remember: Am I not my Brother's keeper? And I remember that no person raises his hand against himself unless he be possessed by Beelzebub, and that it is my Christian duty to help keep safe my Brother's immortal soul, lest he fall into the clutches of the Evil One for eternity." I glance at Fabiola, pretty satisfied with myself. "Do unto others, ah?"

Fabiola sobs. Her face is dark red, and it is scrunched up real ugly. Her lips are stretched back so her teeth show. Scotty Scary.

"¿Qué te pasa?" I say harshly.

Fabiola cries harder. She shakes her head, refusing to

answer. The surge of her breasts inside her jumpsuit is very distracting.

I stop at a roadside stand, buy some unconsecrated wine. "Here," I say, trying to sound solicitous, "drink this."

Fabiola shakes her head.

"Go on," I say, unable to keep my growing anger down. "You'll feel better."

She takes the wine without enthusiasm, swallows twice. I am pretty sure she does it only to shut me up, but so what? The wine seems to settle her.

I speak more gently this time. "Tell Juan Bautista what the matter is."

She says nothing.

"Maybe I'm being a little selfish, but I don't think you have a right to break down in the middle of a shift with absolutely no explanation."

Juanita Rosado chimes us.

"Disciple Five-Four, this is Prophet. Reported double jumper at Morro Bridge. Can you handle? Amen."

Fabiola huddles against the passenger hatch, tight-lipped, red-eyed, shrunken.

I go back to sounding solicitous. "Do you want me to request a substitute unit?"

She shakes her head, and begins feeding data into the brain.

"Are you sure you feel up to handling this?" I say.

Fabiola closes her eyes and nods. She lights her throat mike.

"Prophet, this is Disciple Five-Four," she says in a normal

voice. "We're on our way. ETA is one minute, thirty-seven. Amen."

"Bless you, Five-Four. Amen."

And handle it she does, cool, calm, professional, even though this jumper tried to take her baby with her.

Can you believe it? I wish I could be there when they resurrect that woman, so I could break her face.

14

Fabiola says, "That was my mother."

Today, Fabiola pilots. I need practice running the other half of team duties—communications and computing. I look up from where I am working my way through a biblical-knowledge training program I have to master if I hope to get promoted.

"Who?" I say.

"The woman under the bullet train last month."

"She was your mother?"

Fabiola nods without taking her eyes off the road. I think about what she said.

"Oh," I say.

"That's it?" Fabiola says. "Oh?"

"Hey, I don't know what else to say."

"Mickey Mouth is at a loss for words? Hey, I'm Sammy Surprised."

There is a lot of venom in her voice. Fabiola can be really nasty when she wants to. I notice things like that.

"What do you want me to say?"

"Go with the tried and true, Juan Bautista. Say the first thing that pops into your mind."

"Okay," I say. "How does it feel to know your mother's in Hell?"

I feel a little guilty about that shot, but Fabiola does not react, just continues staring at the road, and drives in silence. At least it shuts her up.

Up ahead, a bustling herd of earthmovers and heavyloaders rumble around construction towers, spidery gantries, and giant mobile cranes. A six-klick-wide swath of torn-up earth is being converted into the magnificent new Estadio José Nicolás Palmer. A swamp of muddy red clay surrounds the huge bowl that is going to seat more than a hundred thousand souls when it is finished. Workfolk in brown builder's jumpsuits swarm over the structure, melding sheets of granite to plasteel girders, hoisting in slabs of smoke-colored marble, shaping enormous semiliquid polyresin molds. They have vowed to work around the clock to complete the project before the End of the World. How is that for true religious devotion? You have to admire that kind of positive attitude.

I switch the dashboard viddy to the news channel.

"—and six days have passed since all contact with Brazilian Mars colony Ribeira Preta abruptly stopped. No explanation for this has been offered. Mars-based emergency teams from the Australian, Japanese, and EuroCom colonies have been dispatched to investigate.

"This is Carlos Calderón, Christian American Capsule News Network."

I wonder what the Devil is going on up there on Mars, and whether the End of the World will come at the exact same instant there and in the lunar villes as it does here on earth. It pretty well has to if every soul that has earned its way into Heaven is going to be called to the Rapture at the same time. Like the song says:

We will all fly to Heaven
When that Glory Morning's done.

I put the Bible quiz back up onscreen, and try to remember why Rahab, who was a harlot of Jericho, is listed in the genealogy of Jesus. I decide to come back to that one, and skip on to the next question: What became of Judas Iscariot's thirty pieces of silver after he hanged himself? That is a snap. The money was used to buy a potter's field for the burial of strangers. I know the one about Shadrach, Meshach, and Abednego, too. I feel pretty proud of myself. I go on working in silence.

Fabiola gives me a scornful look. "My mother's in Hell, you say?"

It takes me a moment to remember what she is talking about. I give her an elaborate shrug.

"She kills herself, she's in Hell. I don't make the rules."

She looks at me with pity and contempt.

"You do a heck of a job comforting the bereaved," she says.

15

"My mother is in Heaven," I tell Angela. "She died giving birth to me."

Evangelios is an intimate Christian youth club with simple religious decorations. A small spectrum unit projects the shadow of a slim cross on the miniature cyclorama behind the stage, while colored lighting effects suggesting stained glass panels play on the other walls. Tiny tables packed with young high church people surround the midget stage. We sip icy alcohol-free fruit drinks—piña coladas and apple-banana punches, mango daiquiris and frozen limon-adas—in tropical oranges, yellows, scarlets, and greens, while a trio called Jesús, María y José performs an acoustic rumba flamenca version of "Cristo Te Ama." Angela and I share a table in back. The lightly bitter scent of incense per-fumes the air.

"And my father's a high muckety-muck in the District of

Christ," I say. "He's allowed to stand in the presence of the Shepherdess, which makes him pretty right-hand-of-God, I guess."

"What's his name? Maybe I've heard of him."

"Oh, you've heard of him, all right. But . . . I'm not supposed to tell anyone."

"Okay." Angela gives me a reassuring smile and turns her attention to the singers.

I feel guilty as sin.

"You and I made a vow, didn't we?" I say.

Angela glances back at me. The hot Gypsy rhythm has seeped into her, and she is dancing in her seat. The quizzical look on her face tells me she has forgotten what I was talking about.

"To trust each other," I remind her. "No secrets."

She smiles and shakes her head. Her dark curls bounce. She has got a great face. Like my mother had.

"That's okay," she says, and I know she means it.

"No, it's not," I say. "I'm sorry." I take a deep breath and plunge in. "My father's the Reverend Jimmy Divine."

Angela's enormous green eyes get even bigger. "Jimmy Divine?" she says. "I guess he *is* pretty right-hand-of-God." She looks at me doubtfully. "But then why is your last name Lorca?"

"That was my mother's name. Brother Jimmy's a Celibate."

I do not know why I feel the need, but before she can speak again, I start bragging about him.

"He personally saved my mother's soul," I say. "He

spotted her dressed as the Blessèd Virgin in an Easter procession and Chose her. Some of our holiest men do that, you know, pick out a young girl from the gutter and minister to her spiritual needs."

"Oh, Sammy Sure, I know about that." Is that a blush on her cheeks, or just the effect of the color filters on the lights? Her brow furrows. "How often do you see him?"

This is the part I hate, because it is so hard to explain. Or maybe it is not so hard to explain. Maybe it is just hard to get people to believe it.

"I've seen him only once in person," I say unhappily. "But I see him every week on *It's Jimmy Divine Time!* I was just a five-year-old crèche kiddy the time we met. What did I know about anything? He explained why his position doesn't allow him to acknowledge me publicly or help support me, and I told him I understood."

Leaving it there always sounds lame to me, so I quickly add, "He said that God has big plans for me."

"Ooh! That sounds exciting!"

"Yeah. But still..."

"What?"

"Well...I know he saved my mother and that anger is a sin, but I still feel he's kind of, you know, a Silas Shithead." My heart pounds just from having spoken those words.

> Cristo te ama, aleluya,
> ¡Aleluya!

Jesús, María y José bow, and Angela and I join in the enthusiastic applause. Before it dies completely, they swing into another song. This time it is one of those really fast merengues from the Dominican Republic they call a perico ripiáu.

> *Oh, they tell me of a land far across the sea,*
> *Oh, they tell me of a land far away,*
> *Oh, they tell me of a land where the wind blows free,*
> *Oh, they tell me of an unclouded day.*

"But he told you God has plans for you," Angela says.

"So?"

She gives me that sweet smile that lights up her whole face.

"So trust in God, dearest Juan Bautista."

16

"Lorca?"

"Presente," I say.

It is a muggy September morning in the squad room of our SPCA station house in Old San Juan. The slogan of the Corps is on prominent display: LA VIDA QUE DIOS QUISO HACER, SOLO DIOS PUEDE DESHACER/THE LIFE GOD MAKES ONLY GOD MAY TAKE. Father Emilio is winding up roll call.

Despite liberal applications of scented disinfectants by the building's maintenance crew, the room still has a faint locker-room smell of sweat and greasy hair and stinky breath, of too many people forced to work too close together in cramped quarters.

The whitewashed ceiling and walls remind me of the smooth shell of a swimming pool. The wooden louvers of the tall, narrow Spanish colonial windows are open. A warm breeze, heavy with sea salt and the stink of sewage, wafts in off the murky harbor waters outside. The smog is so thin today that I can actually make out the coppery span of the Morro Bridge arching over to the foot of the gigantic statue of Christopher Columbus on the Cataño waterfront across the bay. A gift from Russia, the figure towers even higher than the Statue of Liberty in New York Harbor. Twenty-four lanes, and the bridge is still jammed bumper to bumper with early rush-hour traffic. The span looks dull and lifeless in the tired light that manages to filter through the heavy overcast.

"Muñoz?" Father Emilio says.

Fabiola grunts.

Father Emilio is one of my favorite people. I worry about him. He is in his sixties, and he is lugging around a lot more weight than he should on an already chunky frame. What remains of his hair has gone white, and his ample, weathered features give him a fatherly air.

"Rivera?"

"Presente, Father."

The hologram on the far wall unsettles me. There is a sense of holiness and deep spirituality in the life-size reproduction of the Shepherdess bathed in white light, hands upraised in blessing, looking radiant. Yet at the same time, her heavy-lidded eyes, lush lips, and generous breasts—which are lifted into even greater prominence by her upraised arms—seem to send an entirely different message. Maybe it is just me. Okay, it probably *is* just me. This being my marriage year, I find myself seeing lots of things in unexpectedly new and disturbing ways.

"Zambrana?" Father Emilio concludes.

"Presente."

"Okay, squad, let's get out there and save some souls."

We start for the exit, pairing off with our partners or chatting with other squadmates. I tell Nelly Rivera about the hot young guest preacher I saw on *It's Jimmy Divine Time!* last night who asked viewers at home to lay hands on our viddies and help him heal a mute.

Fabiola trails behind, paying us no heed. Out of the corner of my eye, I catch Father Emilio taking Fabiola aside.

"I love *It's Jimmy Divine Time!*" Nelly says. "It's my favorite show. Then *Preacher Pat.*"

"You better hurry if you want to catch up with Luis," I say, stopping in the hallway. "I've got to wait for Fabiola."

Nelly's red curls dance as she jogs away.

"How is the rookie coming along?" I overhear Father Emilio say to Fabiola.

My ears prick up.

"Lorca?" Fabiola says. "The kid has got a lot of growing up to do yet."

Danny Depression. I thought I had started to earn my way up in her estimation. Maybe I should request a new partner. Nelly Rivera? That would be nice, but she is a rookie like me, and you have to team with a vet your first year.

"Pero, ¿quién sabe?" Fabiola says. "He may have possibilities."

Michael Misjudgment! I feel like darting back inside and planting a big wet one on Fabiola's cheek.

"Well," Father Emilio says, "if anyone can make a good one out of him, it's you."

I scoot down the hall and duck around the corner. Wish I knew how to throw a handspring.

17

We are patrolling a stretch of beach road out Vacia Talega way. Traffic is dense. This far from the heart of the city there is no reserved lane, so I have to concentrate on piloting through the crush of cars.

This is nothing like the protected private stretch of Isla Verde beach, where tourists and high churchers gambol. Near the shore in this area, raw sewage stains the Atlantic brown. Turds and worse bob about. Sickening. Even the foam looks filthy. Farther out, as the sea bottom drops off, the ugly brown gives way to the deep blue God intended.

The landward side is real Penny Poverty. Tumbledown shacks cobbled together from weatherbeaten scrap lumber and rusty sheets of corrugated zinc. Mobs of hungry, ragged people surging along the broken slidewalks and spilling into the cratered streets. Abandoned vehicles, stripped and rusting. Starving dogs, bones straining against mangy skin. The stink of open sewers. A real hellhole.

Fabiola says, "Do you still want to marry me?"

Huh? Where did that come from?

"I'm already married," I say uneasily. "Angela and I got married the day after Beverly Bitch jumped off the Morro Bridge with her daughter in her arms."

A long silence.

Halfway to the horizon, a hovertug hauling a train of tanker barges filled with drinking water for Saint Thomas tests its foghorn. The distant Klaxon makes a mournful lowing sound, like a dying cow.

"A little fickle, aren't you?" Fabiola says.

"Hey, Dora Dillydally, you took a long time to 'think about it,' ah? Things change."

"Yes." She nods thoughtfully. The foghorn moans again. "Things change."

We drive. The silence seems very loud. I can make out the hum of the Chevyota's flywheel and the purr of a dirigible swimming through the smog overhead. The hovertug, however, is starting to disappear over the horizon, and its expiring moo has moved out of earshot.

I pull off the road next to a rough-hewn wooden beach stand painted green, yellow, and red. It has a thatched roof made of palm leaves. Tourists love that picturesque kind of stuff. The scrawny vendor has a battered face and a gap-toothed grin. Tourists probably find him picturesque, too. He plucks two green coconuts from an ice locker for me, hacks off their tips with a machete, and slips a straw into each one.

I do not know if she will appreciate the gesture, but I offer one to Fabiola. She lowers her window, and takes it. I lean against her door, and we both suck on our straws. The coconut milk tastes cold and sweet.

"Mmm!" I say. "Isn't this stuff great?"

Fabiola stares into the distance. "Life wasn't always like it is now, you know," she says.

I look up. "Are you talking to me?"

She shakes her head, but goes on speaking. "When my mother was a child, state and church were separate by law. There were multitudes of faiths, and you could believe in whichever one you chose. Or choose to believe in none at all. But the Christian Alliance put a stop to that."

"Hallelujah," I say. "It's Hilda Historian."

She finally looks at me. "God's Rule isn't much older than you are, though your generation thinks that it has always existed." It is like she is another person.

"People are still free to choose their faith," I say. "There are the Christian Jews, the Christian Muslims, the Christian Buddhists, the Christian *everythings*. Our faith has many mansions. You can be any kind of Christian you like."

"Then why have the real Jews, the real Muslims, the real Buddhists, the real 'everythings' all gone underground?"

Is this some kind of stupid riddle? "What do you mean, underground?"

"I mean they still exist, only not out in the open. All

those conversions when the Christian Alliance came to power, you think they were genuine? You think they were voluntary? You think all those millions of people saw the light at the same time because God suddenly decided to illuminate their souls?"

"That was the Great Miracle of the twenty-first century!" I say indignantly. "It's in all the history books. The Christian Alliance saved this country from utter perdition."

My cheeks burn. I take a deep breath, strain to keep my voice calm and even.

"And what was wrong with taking the Word of God to those heathens?" I say. I mean, who does she think she is talking to? "When you have the truth, you're not supposed to keep it your own little secret. It's your Christian duty to share it. Everybody knows that."

Fabiola squeezes her lips into a bloodless line.

"All those converts thanked the Alliance," I say—a little angrily, I have to admit, but, really, can you blame me? "I've heard them. We studied the recordings in Basic Theology."

I wish my voice would not get so strident when I get excited. I sound so Katie Kiddy.

"What the Alliance has imposed is not the natural order of things," Fabiola says slowly. "Nor is the Alliance all that it pretends to be."

"Hey, okay, I know you must be upset about your mother, but I don't like to hear talk against God's Rule." I give Fabiola a really cold look, but she does not notice.

"People have always killed themselves," she says.

"Throughout all of history. Usually because death seemed more attractive than the life they were leading. But it was never like this."

Fabiola's low, self-assured voice and quiet intensity are more intimidating than if she shouted.

"We're just one unit, and we deal with seventy to a hundred self-inflicteds a month," she says in an almost pleading tone. "One unit, Juan Bautista. Every month. Think about it."

A gaunt boy with a bloated belly peeps out from behind a palm tree. He stares at us with shameless hunger, hoping to get our leftovers. Fabiola bites her lip.

"It's a hard, harsh world, overcrowded and dying," she says. "It's not a world people want to live in."

"You sound real Naomi New Christer," I say angrily. Where is she going with this?

"You don't like dealing with uncomfortable ideas, do you?" she asks. She looks me up and down like she does not think much of what she sees. "Or with what might be the truth."

"That's not the truth I know," I say stiffly.

Who is she to judge me? I cannot imagine having wanted to marry this woman. We are totally different. I am ashamed of the lust that blinded me to her true nature.

She sighs. She toys with her straw.

"No, I suppose not," she says. "People are malleable. Young people especially so."

The ocean sits at low tide. The only sound is the intermittent slap of wavelets on the sand nearby. The familiar damp tang of salt air and seaweed surround us.

"If you feel this way, why did you join the Corps?" I ask.

"I didn't always feel this way," she says. "When I joined the Corps, I thought I was performing a holy service. Do you know that feeling? I was proud to be a soulsaver. No one's faith was stronger, no one's loyalty deeper."

She considers the gaunt boy, whose huge eyes never leave her, then takes a deep breath, like she is about to plunge into ice water.

"I even turned in my husband because I suspected him of anti-Christian activities."

I do not think my jaw actually drops, but I feel as though it had.

"I was idealistic and naive, and I thought I had found the handle." She grimaces. "Can you imagine? I thought I had found the handle. I suppose I was a lot like you are now."

Fabiola holds out her empty coconut to the poorboy. He stares at her, his eyes dull, tired. She extends the coconut toward him again. He looks distrustful, but suddenly scurries over, snatches it, and darts away, like he is afraid she is teasing or might take it back. Watching us out of the corner of his eye, he cracks the nut open against the edge of the broken slidewalk. He digs out the rich, thick white pulp inside with his dirty fingers and sucks them clean with loud, juicy slurps.

Fabiola says, "I used to be that kid."

"I'm stunned," I say. "I thought your husband had died."

"Oh, he died all right. They made it look like a suicide, the kind you can't resurrect. Like they did with my mother."

Fabiola coughs. Her lungs sound thick with phlegm.

"That is what will probably happen to me."

Suddenly, I am scared of Fabiola. But I do not want her to know.

"Ah, Cristo," I say disgustedly. "Pamela Paranoid."

Fabiola gives me a wry smile, like we share some special secret.

"What the Herod," she says. "I would think the same thing in your place. I told you I was once young and malleable too, Juan Bautista."

"¡Oye, mira!" the poorboy calls.

We glance over at him. With a smile that is missing a number of teeth, he touches his heart and points at Fabiola, thanking her. Then, for no reason I can fathom, he gives me the finger and runs away.

"You make friends fast," Fabiola says. I do not much care for the smirk on her face.

Fabiola looks away, sighs. A sudden gust of wind brings the smell of rain and the rumble of distant thunder. On the horizon, where the sea melts into the sky, massive black thunderheads race before the wind. Lightning crackles. Rain sheets into the darkening Atlantic.

"Looks like a storm is coming," I say.

"Soulsaver, save thyself," Fabiola whispers so softly I almost miss it.

"¿Qué?" I ask.

"Perdón," she says. "I'm going through a difficult time, and I'm feeling sorry for myself."

She looks hard into my eyes, like there is something she wants to find there but cannot.

"I suppose you'll report me to Father Emilio," she says. She does not sound especially concerned.

"No, I won't."

She nods skeptically.

"I *won't*," I say.

She nods again. "Okay," she says.

18

And I do not. Not to the squad padre. I go right to the top, to the division chief, Archbishop Malpica. That same afternoon. Just as soon as we get debriefed and check out.

The top half of the door to the archbishop's office frames a stained glass panel depicting Jesus weeping in the Garden of Gethsemane. So powerfully does it capture the agony Our Savior must have endured that terrible night that it knots up my throat and dampens my eyes.

I face the archbishop across an eighteenth-century Spanish desk hewn from slabs of dark, ironlike ausubo wood. A terminal screen is built into the desktop. Next to it stands a polished mahogany bowl of apples. Some of the shiny red fruit is stained with dark blotches. Plaques, ornate diplomas, and framed proclamations honoring the archbishop cover three walls. The one directly behind him displays the same life-size hologram of the Shepherdess that graces our SPCA squad room, only this one looks crisper and more lifelike. And a lot more sensual.

Malpica listens to my story with great interest, nodding thoughtfully. I can tell he understands completely. At the end of our interview, he rises to accompany me to the door. I appreciate the courtesy.

White-haired, short, and balding, the archbishop must be well into his sixties. His dark brown face and deep brown eyes project the same sweet, fatherly air I find so simpático in Father Emilio. Unlike Father Emilio, though, the archbishop has to crane his neck to look up at me. He is just a little guy. I tower over him.

"We are very pleased you have brought us this information," the archbishop says.

His habit of touching you to emphasize a point makes you feel he is taking you into his confidence.

"I am a good friend of your distinguished father and you may rest assured that he will be informed of your valuable contribution."

I am shocked. "How do you know who my father is?"

The archbishop gives me a jolly smile. His broad nose crinkles up, and his chubby brown cheeks shine.

"Your father asked me to watch over you many years ago," he says, giving my forearm a reassuring squeeze. "I have followed your progress closely since you were a child."

He reaches a tiny hand up to my shoulder, pulls me down toward him confidingly. His skin gives off the bitter smell of incense. His breath broadcasts the news that he ate arroz con pollo with peas and sweet red peppers for lunch.

"Did you never think to question the ease with which you were accepted in the Corps?"

I stare at him. He winks.

"Well, I'm not doing it for my father," I say quickly. Why do I sound so angry? "I'm doing it because it's *right*."

"You are a young man of staunch and admirable conscience. We take note of that fact, and commend you."

"Muchísimas gracias, su eminencia." Aside from thanking him, I do not know what else I should do.

The archbishop extends his hand to indicate our meeting is over. I genuflect and kiss his ring of office. Even down on one knee, I am almost as tall as he is.

"Go in peace, my son," he says. "And bless you."

The archbishop clasps his hands over his hard little belly. He looks pleased.

I should feel good, too. I have done what is best for Fabiola. The archbishop will see that she gets the proper counseling and aid in setting her life in order, and in the end she will thank me. Greta Grateful.

But instead of basking in a warm, righteous glow as I had expected, I keep thinking about the crazy things Fabiola said.

Because I feel like I missed something, you know?

19

Go tell it on the mountain
Over the hills and everywhere,
Go tell it on the mountain
That Jesus Christ is born!

My headband is tuned to W-G-O-D's '*Round-the-Clock Top Hot Gospel.* The heavy Dominican bachata beat is hard to resist. We are parked on the crest of a hill, the city lights below strung out like rosary beads. Whenever a vehicle passes, my eyes are drawn to the Visage of Christ decals on its headlamps showing that the Lord lights the Way. Those were optional when I was a kiddy, but today every manufacturer includes them as standard equipment. We sure have come a long way.

Across the road, an old vendor everyone calls Don Efraín charcoals shish kebab. Fabiola and I sit in the van's cockpit eating lightly burnt chunks of nu-meat and drinking cold J. C. Cola. The eats are nowhere near dorm-food quality, but Don Efraín's heavenly sauce more than makes up for it. Considering you cannot get real animal flesh outside special church facilities like my dorm or expensive restaurants like El Paraíso de Sushi Número Tres, the food is actually pretty good. Like they say on the viddy: Better living through chemistry.

Fabiola says, "You didn't report me to Father Emilio."

That catches me completely off guard. "¿Qué?" I say.

Billy Brilliant. Does she know about my visit to the archbishop?

"Pues claro que no," I say, trying to recover smoothly. "I told you I wouldn't, and I don't lie."

"Yeah, I have to give you that, Lorca. You are a real straight-and-narrow." She sounds sincere.

"Well . . . thanks," I say.

An awkward pause. I clear my throat.

"I'm sorry about your mother."

Fabiola looks at me suspiciously. "Well, I appreciate your saying so," she finally says.

We eat in silence.

"What do you think about the Twin Messiahs?" she says.

Catches me off guard again. What is she up to? I decide to play along, report anything important to the archbishop.

"Are you talking about the New Christer Cult?"

"Sí. The Followers of the Twins."

"The Twins are profetas falsos," I say. Fabiola's eyebrows shoot up dubiously. "The Shepherdess said so."

Let Fabiola answer that.

"Isn't that what los Fariseos said about Jesus?" she says.

"That is not the same thing," I say hotly.

"Naw, it couldn't be," she says. "History never repeats itself."

"That is exactly what the Shepherdess says," I say.

"Kind of screws up the possibility of that Second Coming we've all been waiting for then, doesn't it?"

Fabiola gnaws at her shish kebab, her face aglow with mock innocence. I sit there frozen.

"You're a New Christer, aren't you?" I whisper. The thought takes my breath away.

Fabiola gulps nu-flesh, washes it down with a swig of J. C. Cola. "I don't know if I'd go that far," she says, "but I'll admit I *have* heard things."

"What things?"

"Cures."

"Cures? You mean like making the blind to see and the lame to walk? Big Dicky Deal. My father does that. On television. Sundays at nine; eight Central."

"Oh, yes, your secret father. 'Heeee-e-e-re's *Jimmy!*'"

I wish I had not told her. Sometimes I think I talk too much. "What about him?"

Fabiola cocks her head to one side, looks at me askance. "Didn't it strike you funny that your dad, 'the Greatest Television Faith Healer of Our Time,' couldn't cure the Shepherdess's daughter when she was dying of leukemia?"

That is the ammunition she has? I laugh inside.

"God told him not to, because He wanted her in Heaven with Him. Everybody knows that."

Fabiola's eyes widen in mock surprise. "Wasn't that *convenient!*"

That kind of talk gets my dander up. "Are you calling my father a Larry Liar?"

Fabiola's eyes narrow. Her face hardens. "I have a son in California," she says. "Juan José. Twelve years old. A sweet little boy. Ana de los Ángeles, my late husband's sister, takes care of him for me. A few months ago, the médicos gave up on him. Van Veerhoeven's sarcoma."

I do not recognize the disease.

"It's an incurable form of brain cancer," she says. "They tried radiation, drugs, chemicals, lab-tailored antiviruses, gene therapy, golden bullets, experimental crap nobody would want inside of them. Nothing worked. And they can't grow you a new brain like they can a heart or lung or kidney. It was, as you truly righteous kiddies so eloquently put it, Harvey Hopeless."

I feel sorry for the little guy. I had no idea Fabiola even had a kiddy.

"What happened?" I say.

"A friend arranged for my sister-in-law to take Juan José to the Twin Redeemers. The girl, Emma, cured him."

"You're saying this little girl, one of the Antichrists, performed a miracle?"

"By their fruits shall ye know them."

"I don't believe you." The archbishop will hear of this heretical chatter pronto.

Fabiola shakes her head. "O, ye of little faith." She gives me a hard look. "Hey, Juan Bautista. I don't lie, either."

I hold her gaze without flinching. But it takes an effort. I try a little humor.

"Tessie Trustworthy," I say.

Not even the glimmer of a smile. I slip a chunk of shish kebab off its skewer and start chewing.

Fabiola says, "And that's the gospel truth, rookie."

I bite into a clove of garlic. It stings my tongue.

20

Following a late morning Sunday Mass, Angela and I head for El Paraíso de Sushi Número Tres. Número Tres is crammed with tiny round tables. The rows of ceiling fans whirling lazily overhead do little to thin the clouds of steam from the kitchen. Or to chase away the wonderfully delicious smells of real food cooking—beef and pork and chicken and rice quick-frying in searing hot woks, fish and vegetables steaming in bamboo baskets.

Business is slow—only seventy-five, maybe eighty, customers this early. What a relief! We have beaten the lunch-hour rush. Número Tres will be jam-packed in another hour or so, but for now we have the place practically to ourselves. Our waiter is Gedde, a Christian Shintoist with chopped bleached hair and a heavy Japanese accent.

"You come for usual?" Gedde says, grinning hospitably.

Gedde's skinny frame barely fills his kimono. On the back of his robe, some street artist has painted the Eye of God. Its silver pupil emits a thin ray of light, illuminating the universe.

"Fine by me," I say. "Angela?"

"Sammy Sure."

"¡Muy bien!" Gedde says.

His bony fingers dance across the input dots of his pocket terminal. Gedde is recently arrived from Okinawa and finds everything here exciting. He is learning to speak English and Spanish, and often mixes the two in a Japanese-accented Spanglish that is kind of cute.

"Two Deruxe Sushi Prate, ¡sí! ¿Vino?" His handling of both languages needs work, but you have to admire him for trying. The only things I can say in Japanese are *Domo ari-gato, Doi toi maeshte,* and *Sayonara.*

Angela shrugs and nods. "Sammy Sure," I say.

"What kind, ¿por favor?"

"Why don't you surprise us, Gedde?" I suggest.

"¿Una sorpresa? My preasure."

It is hard to believe that the levels of mercury and other toxic chemicals in the raw fish we eat today killed people only a century ago. Humans can develop a tolerance for almost anything, I guess. It is just one more proof that God watches over the Crown of His Creations, one more quiet example of the hand of a master designer.

Sunday lunches are the only chance Angela and I get now to spend time together and talk. Since my squad rotated to the night shift, her work-and-sleep schedule and mine do not coincide. But we both still get the Sabbath off. For now.

"You've seemed kind of tired and ... distant these past few weeks, Juan Bautista," Angela says. "You hardly talk with me anymore. I have no idea what you're feeling or what's on your mind."

I know I have not been myself lately, but I did not realize it was so obvious.

"I haven't been sleeping as much as I should," I admit. "And I guess I've had a lot on my mind."

"What's the Tommy Trouble?"

She says it too casually, so I know she has been aching to ask. I *have* had a lot on my mind—new ideas I would never have thought of on my own, new slants on old ideas. Plus the archbishop says it is vitally important to find out how deep Fabiola is in with the New Christers.

Sometimes Fabiola says things that at first sound blasphemous or heretical, but sneak up on you later, prey on your mind. Before you know it, they start to make a weird, unexpected kind of sense, though they go against things I have been taught are true since I was a baby. The fact is that the world seems not so solid anymore. I feel uneasy all the time, belly roiled, brain swarming with contradictions and doubts.

I do not dare tell Angela. She will think my faith is no stronger than a leaf in the wind. Cristo, and I used to compare it to a mighty oak.

"No trouble," I say. "Just work. We're getting so blessèd many self-inflicteds lately. And then there's the stories you hear."

"What stories?" She worries her lower lip between her teeth. "About the Twin Messiahs, you mean?"

Angela is even brighter than I thought. Or maybe I am easier to see through.

"The Calvin Cures? The Molly Miracles? Those stories?" she says. "You know they're all lies."

"I know," I say quickly. "But what about all the people who buy into those lies? Gary Gullibles."

"God is testing us," Angela says gently. "It is all part of His Plan for the Final Days."

That simple, no need to brood on it. Why can't I be like that? Or go back to being like that? I was sure a lot happier then.

"You remember studying how at the close of the twentieth century people thought Christ would return come the year 2000?" Angela asks. "And how when the millennium rolled by and the world kept on ticking, people took it hard and the suicide rate started climbing?"

"Yeah?" I say.

"The buzz at my bureau is that the Shepherdess's team of theologians from the Center for the Study of the Apocalypse has wrapped up that major biblical research project everybody has been waiting on."

"The one about the End of the World?"

Angela nods. "And guess what?" She leans forward and whispers excitedly. "They have proved that earlier calculations were based on faulty Bible translations that threw off the results by a whole blessèd century!"

"*Wo!* Maxie Mistake."

"The true millennium will occur at midnight, December 31st, the Year of Our Lord 2099!" Angela leans toward me, drops her voice even more. "In just six weeks, Juan Bautista! Aren't you excited? The Rapture is coming!"

I spot Gedde approaching. "So is our sushi."

"The official announcement is due this week," Angela whispers quickly.

With great attention to traditional ceremony, Gedde places our orders on the table, positioning each shiny rectangular plate just so. Each plate displays a variety of raw fish and rice balls artfully arranged to form a cross. He awaits our reaction.

"Very beautiful," I say.

Gedde looks at Angela. "Ver' beaurifur?" he says.

"Muy bello, Gedde."

"Taste good, too." He presents his choice of wine. "Serect something muy especial for you."

"Blue Nun?" I say.

Gedde waggles his eyebrows as he quotes the wine's current advertising slogan: "A bressing in ever' bottle!"

21

"You must dissemble, my son," Archbishop Malpica says.

Doesn't *dissemble* mean to lie? But the archbishop would not ask me to sin.

"Pretend to believe your partner's Godless lies. Discover with whom she meets, who her group's leaders are, and, most important, where the twin Antichrists are hiding."

He leans forward and lowers his voice. Such serenity is the mark of a deep spirituality.

"We came very close to capturing them in California," he says, "but they were warned and somehow managed to elude the squad of Avenging Angels that raided the church of that renegade Jesuit who was sheltering them in Santa Cruz. And now"—the archbishop makes a sweeping gesture that takes in the whole world—"they could be anywhere."

He looks at me expectantly.

I do not know what he wants to hear, do not know what I should say, but something is churning up my mind, and this is what comes out.

"I . . . don't feel . . . right about what I'm doing." My heart is pounding. My skin feels clammy. "I feel like I'm some kind of . . . traitor."

The archbishop's forehead furrows with concern. He *cares* about me.

"No, no, my son. She and the other so-called New Christers are the traitors. It is they who betray Our Lord."

"I can't help it," I say. I hate not measuring up to the archbishop's opinion of me. "I feel dirty, like I'm living a lie. Isn't there some other way?"

I notice an overripe scent rising from the bowl of apples on the archbishop's desk. His housekeeper should have put out fresh ones. The thick fruity smell reminds me I have not eaten.

"Your feelings do you honor," the archbishop says. "You are a good man, that is clear."

He smiles. I should smile back, but I cannot.

"I'm weak," I say. "And frightened. And I really don't want to do this."

I cannot just quit on the archbishop. But if I can make him understand the Hell I am going through, he will let me off the hook. Priests have to forgive you. It is in their job description.

Malpica does not look Howie Happy.

"Do you recall what transpired in the Garden of Gethsemane on the eve of the Crucifixion?" he asks.

His eyes are on the glowing stained glass panel behind me. There our Savior kneels, agonizing over the ordeal ahead, seeking guidance from His Father. The men who are supposed to be closest to Him—Peter and James and the other disciples, weak vessels all—nap in blissful ignorance under thorny rosebushes, with no thought to their Lord's fear and pain.

"I remember," I say.

"Our Lord Himself asked His Father if there was not some way His cup might be passed. Our Lord, too, was human and weak. Like you. Or me. But when the time came, what did He say? Do you recall Our Lord's words?"

"I . . . yes."

Tenderly, the archbishop says, "Then, speak them."

"I . . . Thy will be done."

"Can we do less?"

His eyes brim with tears of compassion for me. I cannot let this good man down.

"Again."

"Thy will be done." It comes easier.

Two fat tears roll down the archbishop's shiny round cheeks.

"Feel them in your heart."

"Thy will be done!"

"*Mean* them."

"*Thy will be done!*"

This is what they mean when they talk about being touched by the Grace of the Lord. It feels good. It feels good, good, *good!*

"You stand among the Elect, my son," Archbishop Malpica says. "Take with you our blessing."

He traces the Sign of the Cross over me.

I drop to my knees and plant a heartfelt kiss on the ring that encircles his third finger.

"Thy will be done," I whisper fiercely.

22

Viddy techs swarm everywhere, rigging the studio for recording. Levicams float through their programmed shot list. Tiny fresnels, leakos, scoops, and spots perform an intricately choreographed dance on the light grid high above the soundstage. Controlled by the chief gaffer's wrist terminal, they crisscross, pan, tilt, zoom, filter, focus, and barndoor themselves. Grips float in holoscenery from a huge construction shop next door. Soundmen rig performers with invisible microphones. Gofers go for whatever it is gofers go for. Puts me in mind of the delivery dock at San Francisco—a turmoil of efficient activity that only *seems* like a madhouse.

Angela and I have been watching the preparations for the show from the wings, shivering a little from the chilly air-conditioning. Do they really need to keep it this cold in the studio? I suppose it must get pretty hot under the lights otherwise. A young woman about our own age approaches. She has a mane of flaming red hair, and a body whose voluptuousness even her modestly cut garments cannot completely conceal.

"Sarah?" Angela says, surprised. Is it the bright lights, or does she suddenly look a little pale?

"Angela?" the redhead says with a different kind of surprise. Her skin is so white, I cannot tell if she has paled as well.

"You two know each other?" I ask with yet a third sort of surprise.

"Yes," Angela says, smiling warmly now. "Yes, we do."

Sister Sarah nods enthusiastically, her thick, springy hair bouncing. "We were crèche sisters at the Orfelinato de la Virgen del Pozo."

"You're both from Sabana Grande?" I ask.

I have heard of the Orfelinato, because it became my mother's home after the Quake of '63, the one they call la Madre de los Terremotos, leveled her caserío, crushing her mother and father in the rubble. How a toddler not yet three could have survived such mad destruction is a miracle in itself, a clear sign she had been touched by the Finger of God. I did not know that my mother and Angela shared a similar background and upbringing, or that they had both grown up in the same small town near the southwestern tip of the Island.

"What are you doing here?" Angela asks Sarah.

"I'm the Reverend's personal assistant now," Sarah says,

looking down modestly, as though the post were of no importance. I notice, though, that out of the corner of her eye she is gauging Angela's reaction.

The dizzying heights to which her friend has risen seem to take Angela's breath away. "Oh, well." She looks at me blankly for a moment. "Isn't that something?" she says, almost to herself. She nudges me with a sharp elbow. "Don't just stand there, Juan Bautista. Congratulate my friend."

I smile politely. "Congratulations, Sister Sarah. You must be very proud. In a humble sort of way, of course."

"Yes, thank you, I *am* humbly proud." Sister Sarah glows with pleasure. She turns to Angela. "And you?"

"Me? I'm married now and expecting," Angela says, slipping her arm through mine. "This is my husband, Juan Bautista Lorca."

Sister Sarah says, "Oh, my." She looks askance at Angela. "You're the couple who are here to see the Reverend?"

Angela tightens her grip on my arm and nods slowly.

"Well, in that case," Sister Sarah says, suddenly all friendly efficiency, "please come this way."

She leads us onto the set. I cannot help noticing how flatteringly her robes cling to her body, though Angela's sleeker curves are more to my liking. At the center of the set, a smoke fountain gushes out cascades of fake fog. A florid, beefy six-footer with twinkling blue eyes strides through the clouds, white hair and beard neatly trimmed.

"Bless you, boys and girls!" he booms in a Texas accent. "It's all comin' together like a dream!"

My father: the Reverend Jimmy Divine.

The icy chill inside the studio sends a shiver down my spine.

Jimmy Divine spots us and homes in on our group. I feel Nelly Nervous.

Sister Sarah is quick to do the honors. "This is Brother Juan Bautista Lorca, Brother Jimmy."

"You don't have to tell me who *this* is, Sister!" Jimmy Divine says.

"Bless you...," I begin, unsure how I should address him, "uh, Brother Jimmy."

"Bless *you*, Brother Juan," he says.

He is overflowing with vim and vinegar, a guy who is never unsure about anything, like the big man in *She Wore a Yellow Ribbon*. He gives me a crooked grin.

"Correct me if I'm wrong, son," he says in his Lone Star drawl, "but ain't Juan Bautista Spanish for John the Baptist?"

Why does he do that? I had almost started to like him, but now he is acting unbelievably Silas Shithead, pretending not to know the meaning of the name he picked out for me himself. Bitterness boils up inside me.

"You're an educated man, Brother Jimmy," I say through clenched teeth.

Jimmy Divine turns my resentment into a joke.

"Well, I *have* been to Sunday school, you know," he says with a deep-throated chuckle. "And this lovely example of Christian womanhood must be your beautiful young bride! I gotta tell ya," he says, giving her the once over, "she is a dead ringer for your dear departed mother."

"Oh, did you know my mother?" I ask, practically spitting.

"Very well," he says without missing a beat. "Amparito Lorca was a beautiful, saintly woman. Her death was a great loss." He shakes his head sadly. "Only the good die young."

He is a slick one. Charming, too, if you do not know better.

"This is my wife, Sister Angela Amador de Lorca, Brother Jimmy. Angela, my fa—" I am trying to be Carlos Cool, but almost blow it. In my haste to correct myself, I end up stuttering like a blessèd idiot. "I . . . ahm . . . mean the Reverend Jimmy Divine."

Nobody seems to notice my blunder.

"Bless you, Brother Jimmy," Angela says, plainly charmed, but a little nervous too, which is only natural, Jimmy Divine being such a huge and saintly media star. Still, I am surprised someone as bright as Angela does not see through him.

"And bless *you*, Sister Angela," Jimmy Divine says, giving her a friendly wink.

"Can I get you folks anything?" Sister Sarah asks.

"Why, thank you kindly, Sister, that won't be necessary," Jimmy Divine says. "But you *could* give Sister Angela the tin-dollar tour and catch up on old times, while me and Brother Juan do a little catchin' up of our own." Jimmy Divine flashes her that wonderful smile.

Sister Sarah smiles back. "Yes, Brother Jimmy. Please follow me, Sister."

Jimmy Divine eyes Sister Sarah's figure as she walks away. "The Lord has seen fit to bless dear Sister Sarah in

101

many ways," he says with a grin, then sits in a candy-apple-red VIP chair. "It's been a while since *It's Jimmy Divine Time!* broadcast live from this lovely island of yours," he says.

"Why did you summon me?" I ask, not long on patience.

"The show's here only till New Year's, and a father likes to see his son every now and again—as you'll find out soon as you start havin' kids of your own, now you're married."

"You haven't wanted to see me in seventeen years."

"Well, ain't you the blunt one."

He smiles his trademark smile. Hard to be on the receiving end of it and not find yourself liking him.

"That is an uncharitable thing to say, son. Not seein' you and not wantin' to see you ain't nowhere near the same thing at all." He drops a paternal hand on my knee, as if he has done that since I was a kiddy. Which, of course, the smooth bastard hasn't. "I've kept my eye on you, though, son, and gotten real good reports."

He has kept his eye on me?

"Let's face it," he says, "you're a comer, Juan Bautista, and I'm right proud of you!"

"What kind of reports?" I ask.

"Tony Malpica thinks the world of you."

"The archbishop?"

"How many Tony Malpicas do you know?" He is right. The question makes me feel stupid. "So," he asks, "how close are you?"

"Close? To what?"

"To findin' out where they're hidin'." Jimmy Divine sees

the confusion on my face. "The Twins, Emma and Noel," he says with an encouraging look. "Them little heathen Antichrists."

"The Twin Redeemers?" I give a shrug. "I don't know where they are."

"Tony says you're close to findin' out."

I clear my throat. "Well, maybe."

"We need that information desperately, son," he says. "We?" I say.

"The Shepherdess herself is countin' on you. The Antichrists have to be defeated if we're gonna fulfill the prophecies of the Final Days and bring on the Rapture. And they ain't but two weeks left till the End of the World. You are gonna have to move fast."

"The Shepherdess . . . is counting on *me*?"

"We all are, son. The Lord has singled you out, just like I told you he would." He clips the point of my chin lightly with a mock right hook, and flashes me that crooked cowboy grin. "You are a chip off the old block, boy, and I ain't ashamed to tell you I am right proud."

I feel light-headed. I came here angry, heart black toward my father. Now, with only a few words, he has made me feel good about myself. And about him.

"What do I do?" I ask.

"Keep doin' what you been doin'. This partner of yours— Fabiola Muñoz?—we know she's one of them." Jimmy Divine gives me a hearty slap on the knee. "You done a good job of gettin' her to believe you're on the fence, son. But now's the time to let her flat convert you."

Praise from my father? My face grows warm, and my heart beats faster.

"Mind you don't flipflop too easy," he adds. "Wouldn't do to get her suspicious. But don't drag it out neither, y'understand?"

"Then what?"

"Don't you worry yourself about that. When the Lord says the time is right, I'll let you know."

I nod. He stares at me. Is he waiting for something? I have no idea what it could be. Angela rushes up.

"Oh, Juan," she says excitedly, "you've just got to see this place! They've brought everything with them that they show on the viddy: the Little Lord Jesus Healing Nook, the Live a Righteous Life Forever Revival Tent, the Holy Moses Prayer Garden and Wishing Well, even the Hark the Herald Angels Sing Portable Above Ground Baptismal Pool! Ooh, I am just filled to the brim with that old-time religion!"

"Amen, Sister!" Jimmy Divine cries. "I love it when the righteous talk like that."

He puts his long arms around us, and draws Angela and me in close, like we are a family.

"You know," he says, "it is gonna be a truly joyous holiday season this year. First, Christmas with you young'uns, then, come midnight New Year's Eve—the Rapture!"

He beams his good-ole-boy grin on us full force.

"And won't that be a sight?" he says. "All the good Christians in the world, the livin' and the returned-to-life, joinin' hands and risin' to Heaven like a flock of homesick angels!"

His sonorous voice fills with awe. "And the world will see the whole thing on *It's Jimmy Divine Time!*—live, with special guest Jesus Christ!"

"Jesus Himself?" I whisper, astonished.

"Back by popular demand." He grins, then elbows me and winks. Oh, a joke. Okay, maybe it *is* funny, but it makes me uneasy. It seems to border on the sacrilegious. Though I guess that could hardly be true, could it? Not coming from someone on Jimmy Divine's spiritual plane.

Sister Sarah interrupts. She has a prompt book in her hand and a no-nonsense look in her eye. "Excuse me, Brother Jimmy," she says, "but you're needed on the set right away."

"Don't let us down now, Juan Bautista." Jimmy Divine leans in till our foreheads touch. "We are countin' on you, boy," he whispers.

Carried away, I say, "I won't let you down, Da—" But Jimmy Divine cuts me off with an impish that's-a-no-no finger wag. He laughs a big booming laugh, then gives Angela what strikes me as an unnecessarily long bear hug that leaves her gasping for breath.

"And I'm lookin' forward to seein' you again *real* soon, little lady!" he says with another wink.

Talk about charm! He even has *me* beaming.

I have never seen her so flustered. "Ahm . . . me too, Brother Jimmy."

It is only natural that she should be a little awed in the presence of someone of Jimmy Divine's nearness to God. But it occurs to me that something else may be at work here as well. Could Angela envy her former crèche sister her exalted position, if only a little? Sure, envy is one of the deadly sins, but nobody is perfect. She may be thinking that if she had been the one to catch Jimmy Divine's eye instead of Sister Sarah, her life might have been different, like it was for my mother.

Jimmy Divine places a big rawboned hand on Angela's belly and says, "So, how's our little fella doin'?" Takes me completely by surprise.

Angela blushes and averts her gaze. "We... don't know if it's a boy or a girl yet, Brother Jimmy."

Brother Jimmy gives a hearty chuckle. "Well, I do know," he says jovially. "That there's a boy, mark my words." He elbows me again, like he is bringing me in on some joke I do not get. "I have a sixth sense about such things, ain't that right, Sister Sarah?"

Sister Sarah smiles politely, and nods ever so slightly at the prompt book in her hands. Jimmy Divine says, "You young folks will have to excuse me for scootin', but it appears this here's to be our last run-through, and I've still got me some miracles to rehearse."

With no warning, he leans down and gives Angela a kiss on the cheek that catches her off guard. She gasps, puts her hand to her mouth, then quickly smiles and says, "Oh, my!"

Jimmy Divine pats her tummy in fatherly fashion. "Now you be takin' real good care of our little fella there, y'hear?"

I cannot say I care for such liberties, even if he is Angela's father-in-law now.

23

Fabiola and I are prepping a dozer in the back of the van. A dozer is an SID who wanted to take the "easy" easy way out, and swallowed a bucketful of sleepies. Dozers look peaceful and happy, like they are catching forty winks and enjoying sweet dreams. They are big favorites at the Resurrection Center. Folks who try to check out the "easy" easy way are the easiest to bring back. No traumatized tissue to restore, no smashed organs to reconstruct or replace, no scattered parts to reassemble. Just some simple brain-cell regeneration and soul recall, and, ¡milagro!, your soulkiller is back in business.

We work in silence. I connect a twin-feed hookup carrying liquid nitrogen and heavy plasma into the ileac vein.

"That child of yours, what was his name, the one with brain cancer?" I ask as casually as I can.

Fabiola's blank face cannot mask the surprise and curiosity in her eyes.

"Juan José," she says after a moment. She gives me a hard look. "What about him?"

I pretend I do not notice the look, and continue as casual as you please. "Is he still cured?"

The liquid-nitrogen compressor bubbles. Plasma oozes through the webweave insertion tube. All Ricky Routine.

"What do you mean, still?" Fabiola asks.

I shrug. "Is he okay, or has he had some sort of, you know, relapse?"

"Ana de los Ángeles says the lab tests not only show no trace of cancer, they show no sign that he ever had it."

Can this be true? It *is* only hearsay. She has no actual proof. I nod, so she will think I believe.

We continue our work in silence. My brain feels stuffed with cotton, and my eyes burn. I could not sleep last night from brooding on how the foundations of faith I always thought so solid have lately turned so shaky. I ask Fabiola something that has been gnawing at me for a long time.

"When did you stop being like me?"

"What do you mean?"

"You called me idealistic and naive. And malleable. And said that you were like that yourself when you were my age. What made you change?"

Fabiola lights the brain scanner. Three short buzzes announce when it is done. The scan is flat. This chica is one dead dozer.

Fabiola logs in and autostamps the readout. She eyes me

speculatively. She cannot possibly suspect my real motive for asking. Or can she? I have to play the rookie seeking wisdom from the wise old vet.

"What made me change?" she says. She rubs her right temple, seems to come to a decision. "It's tough to pinpoint exactly, but I guess I started seeing below the surface of things. And I guess I discovered people aren't always what they pretend to be, and their real motives aren't always the ones they show you. And I guess I started noticing that what they teach you in Sunday school doesn't always jibe with real life."

She sighs, shrugs.

"So I guess what it all boils down to is that maybe I started growing up."

She looks at me hard again. "Why do you ask?"

I hold her gaze. "I guess maybe I'm starting to have thoughts like that myself."

"Ooh, Gary Grown-up," she singsongs, but with a friendly grin. "You ready, Lorca?"

The question catches me off balance. "Ready for what?"

Fabiola nods at the dozer. The nitrogen and plasma feeds are complete. It is ice time.

"All set here, Muñoz," I say.

"Then let us do our duty, Corpsman."

Though we do not speak as we haul the meat to San Francisco, I think I sense a new feeling of camaraderie with Fabiola.

Have we somehow bonded?

24

"It feels good to talk to somebody about these things," I say.

Fabiola understands. We are in tune.

"What about your wife?" Fabiola asks. "Can't you talk to her?"

Traffic is as thick and sluggish as heavy plasma. It oozes.

"Talk to Angela?" I say. "Angela has no doubts. Angela believes, period."

"Sounds like somebody I used to know." Fabiola grins.

"Meaning me?"

"Ricky Right, rookie."

From the looks of the sky, we are in for another dirty sunset. A hundred years ago, the heavens were blue, the clouds were white, the Caribbean sun was a yellow so bright that no one today can imagine it. "El Rubio," folks called the sun: "the Towhead." Now, El Rubio has lost its luster behind the perennial smog, and the sky looks like God smeared shit on it.

"I don't think I'm a rookie anymore," I say quietly.

It suddenly hits me: has Fabiola done her hair differently today? Yes, she is wearing it in a single thick braid instead of pulled back into its usual knot. How come I did not notice before? What else am I missing?

"Maybe you *are* past the rookie stage," she says, matching my tone. "But where did all these doubts come from, Lorca? Why the sudden interest in the Twin Redeemers?"

"I'm not blind," I say. "I see the poverty, the overcrowding, the suffering. And Lord knows I see the suicides." I shake my head in amazement. "So many people who would rather go to Hell than go on living." I notice the doubt in her eyes. "And it's not sudden, either, Muñoz. I've been thinking about this stuff—and other things you've said— for a while."

All on the straight and level. De corazón, right from the heart.

Fabiola just grunts.

How should I read that? How can I persuade her of my sincerity?

"I told you once that I admire you and want to be like you," I say.

Fabiola snorts in disbelief. "And I told you you were crazy."

"I guess I'm still crazy." I say this in a voice as even as I can manage.

Fabiola shakes her head sadly. "I guess you are."

I take a deep breath. Nothing ventured, nothing gained. "I'm looking for answers. I think maybe you've got some."

"You think I've found the handle?" A mock-despairing look. "¿Estás loco, muchachito?"

Have I broken through? "I'm not crazy," I say. "And I'm not some dumb little kiddy." I look her straight in the eye. "And, yeah, I think you've found the handle."

Fabiola studies me, openly taking the measure of what may be a new Juan Bautista.

A subtle softening. Has she decided to believe me?

"You know," she says quietly, "I think maybe this time I have."

25

"We are proud of you, my son."

Archbishop Malpica dabs a heavy linen napkin at a glob of real parcha preserves clinging to the corner of his tiny mouth.

"You have succeeded in earning your heretical partner's trust much faster than we had dared hope. The excellence of your work has been noted and will be rewarded. Felicitaciones."

I say, "Muchas gracias, su eminencia," though my heart is not in it. I am not feeling particularly grateful or gung ho today. My stomach feels as cold and greasy as the untouched huevos en su nido a la vinagreta on my plate.

A few months ago, such praise would have made my day. But something has changed, and I am not sure what. Things look ... different.

"I detect little enthusiasm in you, Juan Bautista. Would you pass the papaya, please?"

I hand the archbishop a cut-glass plate piled high with sweet, golden slices of fruit. I am tired and fretful, with no real appetite, though I should feel honored at the invitation to share this bountiful breakfast with His Eminence.

"I am having bad feelings again about this business," I admit.

Malpica squeezes fresh lime over his melon. Limes— along with lemons, oranges, grapefruit, breadfruit, parcha, mangoes, papayas, bananas, tamarinds, guava, and a cornu- copia of other tropical fruits—were a cash crop in Puerto Rico a century ago, when the population hovered just over the four million mark. But now that the Island has been buried under enough plascrete to provide roads and hous- ing for thirty million souls and counting, almost everything we eat is shipped in from the Mainland or synthesized in the nutrition labs. So the lime slices tell you the archbishop is someone to reckon with. Fresh limes are impossible to come by, unless you are a top-echelon Christian. To say nothing of the other rare treats gracing our table.

The archbishop chews and swallows with great deli- cacy. "Really?" he says. "How so?" He waggles his fingers. "Hand me those raspberries, my son."

The archbishop is projecting that warm fatherly feeling that makes you want to confide in him. But something in the tilt of his head says he does not want to hear what I have to say.

I tell him anyway.

"I feel . . . guilty," I say. "Ashamed. Real Sigmund Sinner, you know? Fabiola trusts me, and I'm going to do her dirt."

"Ah, ah, ah," Malpica mumbles around a mouthful of melon. "You must never think that, my son."

"I can't help it. I'm doing the sort of thing I was taught in Sunday school I shouldn't do."

With my fork I rearrange the food on my plate. The carefully cooked eggs stuffed with chopped tomato, onion, and garlic feel rubbery. The thick slab of toast next to them has sopped up the grease on my plate like a sponge.

"I feel like I'm jumping feet first into Hell," I mumble.

Malpica settles back in his chair.

"We have been through this before, my son," he says patiently. "You are going about the Lord's work. It is the Adversary who whispers these doubts in your ear to weaken your resolve."

I had not thought of that. What else could I have overlooked? "You think so?"

"I have no doubt of it," he says, blotting his mouth with a heavy linen napkin.

This further complicates things. And scares me. "But what can I do?"

"You must follow Our Lord's example, and"—Malpica pauses to swallow a forkful of thin buttery crêpes slathered in whipped cream and chocolate syrup—"do as He did when tempted while fasting for forty days in the desert."

Malpica's lips glisten. He licks them. The tip of his tongue is thick and blunt. "Do you remember His words?" he asks.

"Ahm . . . get thee behind me, Satan," I say halfheartedly.

The archbishop smiles encouragingly. "Do you feel your spirits lifted?"

Is he kidding? A glance at my congealed eggs sends bile into my throat. Oh, Lord, do not let me be sick!

Malpica leaps to his feet.

"Of course not!" he booms. "You must reach within your soul, into the very deepest wells of your faith, and with the mystic strength you draw from there, reject the Evil One!"

He thrusts his face next to mine, like he is going to whisper in my ear, and shouts, "Say it again!"

I jump back, knocking over a very expensive glass of freshly squeezed orange juice. I do not think. I start yelling: "Get thee behind me, Satan! *Get thee behind me, Satan!* GET THEE BEHIND ME, SATAN!"

Malpica gesticulates wildly for me to go on.

"Get thee behind me, Satan! *Get thee behind me, Satan!* GET THEE BEHIND ME, SATAN!"

My heart pounds. My head is bursting. But I do not feel my spirits lifting.

I keep yelling, and the pitch of my voice climbs higher and higher. Soon only dogs will be able to hear me. And here comes Malpica, waddling toward me with a look in his eye that, by God, means business.

With no-nonsense efficiency, he clamps one hand onto the crown of my head and palms my face with the other. The berries and cream on his breath barely mask last night's steak smothered in onions. I try to jerk loose from his suffocating grasp, but he has too strong a grip.

He shoves his face against mine—eye to eye, nose on nose, lips brushing lips—and shrieks, "BEGONE, AC-CURSED ONE!"

My eyes roll up. I see blackness. I go limp.

Malpica releases me.

I fall toward the black-and-white tiled floor.

But never feel myself hit it.

26

The darkness glows.

We lie in our marriage bed, exploring a world where everything is soft, slow, and sensuous.

"Do you like it when I . . . do that?" Angela whispers.

"Ay, sí . . . that's Nicky Nice."

I can still feel the archbishop's tiny hand gripping my face, just large enough to cover my eyes and nose and mouth. I can still feel myself falling.

"And how about when I touch you . . . like this?" Angela says.

"Sí, that's . . . ay, sí."

"You like that, mi amor?"

Thoughts of the archbishop begin to fade.

"You are so sweet, Angela."

"Dios mío, Juan Bautista, would you think me wicked if I . . ."

She whispers in my ear. I pull back.

"¿Desnudos? You want us to make love unclothed?"

"Wouldn't you like that?" She sounds hurt.

"The Lord says it's wrong."

"The priests and the preachers say it's wrong."

"Isn't that the same thing?"

"Is it?"

What is going on? Now even Angela has me questioning things I thought unquestionable. Where will it end?

A rustling sound. "What are you doing?" I ask.

"Slipping out of my marriage robe."

I do not know what to do. I mean, I know what I should do. Rather what I should *not* do. But on the other hand . . .

"But what about the baby?"

I can hear a smile creep into Angela's voice. "The baby can't see us, silly."

"I don't want to hurt it."

"How could making love naked hurt it?"

"I just don't think we should, you know."

Angela molds her body to mine, moves against me. Her swollen belly feels smooth and taut. It reminds me of a wooden carving of a pagan fertility goddess I saw once on a school field trip to the Museum of Pre-Columbian Art on La Caleta de las Monjas in the Old City.

"We are married, Juan Bautista," she whispers. "We are man and wife. Does not the Lord Himself say that a man shall cleave unto his wife, and they shall be one flesh? Do you remember that?"

I find it difficult to swallow.

"Yes. Genesis, chapter two, verse twenty-four."

"And does not Saint Paul say that when a man is with his wife, 'let him do what he will, he sinneth not'? First Corinthians."

"Chapter seven, verse . . . thirty-six."

"Lift your arms now, mi amor."

I do as she says.

"And let me help you slip this . . . off!"

The night slithers across my skin, cool where I have grown moist. My body seems to take up more space. Angela fits herself to it.

"Mmm," she says. "Now isn't this much nicer?"

We begin slowly, searching for a rhythm. I open my eyes. Angela's sweet features glow with delight.

A delight that I put there.

"Angela," I whisper.

"Juan . . ."

I close my eyes. Our lips brush, we come gently together, and tenderly fuse.

27

"Forgive me, Father, for I have sinned."

I kneel impatiently in a sidewalk confessional, shivering in my thin kaftan. I have just established an emergency link to my confessor, Father René.

Outside the booth, a light early-morning sunshower dampens the crowds of passersby slidewalking to work. I have heard that Hawaiians call it "liquid sunshine," but in Puerto Rico there is a different folk belief. Here, rain under a bright sun signifies that "the Witch is marrying the Devil."

Onscreen, Father René looks a mess. His eyes are sleep-puffed and squinty. An overnight growth of beard darkens his cheeks and jaw like soot, and his uncombed hair is like a field of weeds. Yet even though the sun has barely peeked over the horizon, he says nothing to make me feel guilty for waking him at so ungodly an hour. Father René is okay, always there when you need him, a good shepherd watching over his flock.

"Do you know what time it is, Juan?" he mumbles.

"I'm sorry, Father. It can't wait."

All night I've lain awake, afraid to fall asleep for fear the Lord would take me while my soul was in a state of mortal sin, Davey Damned with a one-way ticket to Hell waiting to be punched, the same two lines echoing and reechoing in my brain: *Don't want to die unshriven, Lord. Don't want to die unshrived.*

"Okay, then," Father René rumbles. "What is the nature of your transgressions, my son?"

"I have lain naked with a woman," I mutter.

Father René snaps awake. He blinks four times. "What woman is this, Juan Bautista?"

"Angela," I say. "My wife."

I left Angela in bed, sleeping. She does not know I have come here, does not know I have lain awake all night, fearful God might take me before I could confess and be forgiven. Angela would be upset if she knew. She would think that I blame her.

"There is some confusion here," Father René says, his voice still an early-morning bass. "It is no sin to lie with your wife."

"But Nancy Naked?" I ask. Without our marriage robes?" I feel hot with guilt just saying it. "In Sunday school, they told us that to do so is a sin."

"Well," he says, "there are certain things you are not taught in Sunday school. Viewpoints other than the official one. Some theologians maintain that nudity between husband and wife is a part of the natural order. If we are born unclothed, why should we not also be conceived unclothed?"

"It's not cut-and-dried?" I do not think I like where this is going.

"I believe it is something you must decide for yourself."

Cristo, another new idea. Just what I was afraid of.

"Well, I don't like it," I finally say. "You shouldn't have to think about religion. It should be . . ."

"Carved in stone?"

Father René looks, what, amused? But I like his analogy. "Yes, like the Commandments."

"Do you recall the three preconditions for sin?" Father René asks.

What does that have to do with anything?

"Sammy Sure." What is his point? This is basic Catecismo. "You must know it is a sin," I say. "You must want to do it anyway. And you must do it of your own free will."

Father René nods, pleased with my answer. "So you see," he says, "even sin requires thought. God does not want a race of good little robots programmed not to sin. He wants us to do right because we have made a moral choice, using our head and heart."

Why does this not make me feel any better? "Well, I wish this moral-choice stuff were easier," I say.

Father René smiles ruefully. "Don't we all." His expression turns serious. "But, you see, Juan Bautista," he says in that gentle way he has, "being able to choose is what makes you human. And whether you choose for Evil or for Good is what makes you you."

"I don't know, anymore," I say. Why does it always have to come down to me? "Things were so much simpler when I joined the Corps. I could tell right from wrong then as easily as white from black. But now . . ."

"But now?"

"Black isn't black, and white isn't white. It's all shades of gray."

"Welcome to the world, my son."

"I want things to be like they used to, Father."

Like he has the power to grant that. When am I going to grow up and be a man?

"We all want our innocence returned, Juan," Father René says gently.

"But nobody ever gets it back, ah?"

"Not in this life."

So where does that leave me?

"What should I do?" I say. "There are so many choices to make all of a sudden. How do I decide what's right?"

Father René closes his eyes, massages them with his thumb and forefinger. "Look into your heart," he says.

He traces the Sign of the Cross in the air. "Go in peace, my son."

"Praise the Lord."

"Praise Him."

I disconnect.

Back where I started. On my own again.

28

We crawl through the crowds at Madre Teresa. Everywhere, people. Images from my first soulsaving assignment
replay in my mind, almost identical to the sights outside the
van's windows. Old farts, unemployed teeners, clamoring
beggars, spindle-limbed children, pregnant women, gestic-
ulating street preachers, dull-eyed faithful.

It kills me to have to drive this slowly with the kind of
horsepower our van boasts. A broken-down hulk in the
penance lanes could move faster. Heck, a kiddy on crutches
on a dead slidewalk could move faster. The stink of uncollected months-old garbage overpowers the van's air filters
and makes me gag.

BIENVENIDO AL CASERÍO MADRE TERESA
WELCOME TO THE MOTHER TERESA HOUSING PROJECTS

Speaking of your Denise Déjà Vu, up ahead is the welcome sign. It looks even filthier than I remember. I wonder if we will be getting any Double Jesus chatter now that the cult has been outlawed?

We navigate at practically no kilometers per hour through this petrified forest of identical buildings. Finally, we park in front of one painted in peeling raspberry with cracked white trim.

And I realize we *have* been here before.

This is the same apartment where Fabiola and I found Carmen Colón in her chipped pink bathtub, veins sliced from palm to elbow.

My first SID. You never forget something like that.

It rarely happens among the resurrected, but for an instant I wonder if Carmen has tried to do herself in again.

No such thing. This call turns out to be a café-con-leche-skinned kiddy, dead from a self-inflicted blast dart. Carmen Colón is on the floor, cradling the kiddy's head. The cuts on her forearms have healed nicely. You would not notice them if you did not know where to look. A gaggle of younger children ranging in age from toddler to teener peer at us from the hallway, the bathroom, the kitchen, and the apartment's tiny balcony.

"¿Cómo se llama la víctima?" I ask.

"¡Mi bebé! ¡Mi bebé!" she sobs. "¡Esto es mi culpa! I set you a bad example."

"Señora," I say. She looks at me, eyes swollen, mouth twisted with grief. "The boy's name?" I ask again.

"Carmelo," she moans, making it sound like the saddest name in the world.

"Your son?"

She nods tragically, rocking to some secret rhythm, as if trying to pump life back into her child. Carmelo's brothers and sisters watch out of huge eyes, afraid to venture anywhere near their brother or the strangers who have come to take his body away.

"Don't cry, señora. We'll bring your son back. Se lo prometo."

I had hoped to calm her. Instead, she sobs harder. I do not understand. The smaller children begin crying loudly in sympathy. Their sorrow makes a racket loud enough to wake a corpsicle.

Fabiola ignores the hubbub. She toggles her throat mike and sets to work.

"Preliminary data log: Carmelo Colón. Male. Mulatto. Estimated age eighteen."

The air litter is outside in the hallway. I go for it. The sobbing children step back quietly to let me pass.

"Fourteen," Carmen moans. "My son was only fourteen."

"Correction. Age fourteen," Fabiola says softly. "Self-inflicted death type one."

I squeeze the litter in through the narrow front door. The children cower away from me, the older ones hugging the smaller ones.

"¡Mi pobre bebé!" Carmen wails. "They will freeze you, then call you back to life, and it hurts so much when they wrench your soul from eternity back into your body, your flesh burning from the ice."

She blubbers. The children blubber along with her.

Fabiola and I try to disengage the boy from her arms. Carmen fights us, scratches my neck with her jagged fingernails. I jerk away. Fabiola murmurs in her ear, and the woman suddenly loses heart.

I feel the scratches bleeding, but I do not want the woman to see me touch them to find out how bad they are.

"Loading for delivery." Fabiola toggles her mike off.

I am floating the air litter out when Carmen Colón speaks again.

"And then," she sobs, "they put you on trial and punish you for trying to escape."

I hurry down the hall. I want to get away.

"And then," she calls after me, "and then you are afraid ever to try again."

She and her children weep.

The wounds in my neck sting, but I do not touch them.

29

I slip six tin dollars into the popcorn machine. A container plops into the dispenser. There are words on its side shaped like melted butter that read: O LITTLE TOWN OF BETHLEHEM GIANT KERNEL POPCORN—ANOTHER FINE MANNA-FROM-HEAVEN PRODUCT. Hot, fluffy white kernels overflow it. The smell makes my mouth water.

I buy a second tub, plus a couple of Holy Moses! chocolate bars and J. C. Colas. Music belts out from the rec room speakers, all brass and banjos and ringing tambourines. My dorm mates have crowded in front of the wall screen to watch *It's Jimmy Divine Time!*

> *Give me that old time religion,*
> *Give me that old time religion,*
> *Give me that old time religion,*
> *It's good enough for me!*

Here he comes now!

Jimmy Divine sprints on stage. He leaps, he spins, he drops to his knees, fervently preaching Salvation.

Image splash!

Jimmy Divine grinds his thumbs into the eyes of a blind woman. He screams at the demon possessing her. He shouts Hallelujah when he makes her see.

Image splash!

Jimmy Divine throws back his massive head. He duck-walks across the stage, playing a synthotar shaped like the Cross, singing out of holy exuberance.

Image splash!

Jimmy Divine juggles a rattler six feet long. He jams his nose against the snake's evil snout. He spits in its devil eye.

Image splash!

Jimmy Divine embraces a filthy beggar. He kisses the man on both cheeks like a long-lost brother. On his knees, he washes the mendicant's grimy feet with his own healing hands.

Image splash!

Jimmy Divine lifts up a crippled kiddy, weeping un-ashamedly over the child's affliction. He straightens her legs. She walks again.

Image splash!

Jimmy Divine marches fervidly in place. Behind him, a massive white cross flares blindingly against the night. Head high, he marches. Unstoppable, he marches.

It was good for my father

The brass turns martial.

It was good for my mother

The tambourines give way to kettledrums.

It was good for my brother

Pride in America wells up in your heart, right there alongside your love for Jesus.

And it's good enough for me!

Impelled by some golden vision of Paradise, Jimmy Divine marches, marches on.

I get goosebumps.

A million golden fireflies sweep down from the heavens to shimmer around him. They soar, they shimmy, they swoop together to form vast glowing designs. And suddenly you realize that there, burning across the ebony sky in fiery script of gold, blaze the words we have been waiting for: IT'S JIMMY DIVINE TIME!

With stalwart chin, the recorded Jimmy Divine marches ever onward beneath the blazing Cross of Redemption.

Fog fills the screen.

Brother Conn Darden cries, "And now, Brothers and Sisters, heeeee-e-e-e-re's *Jimmy!*"

The living Jimmy Divine materializes, older and heavier than his prerecorded image, but with a smile ten times more infectious and radiant.

Angela grins. I grin. We all grin.

"Bless you, Brothers and Sisters everywhere!" Jimmy Divine booms.

"Bless you, Brother Jimmy!" we chorus back.

This is exciting and uplifting and fun—everything religion was meant to be.

"Thank you for tuning in the Lord!" Jimmy Divine says. "Who do we love?"

We know the answer to that one.

"Jesus!"

"Who do we love?"

"*Jesus!*"

"Who—do—we—love?"

"JESUS!"

"Amen, hallelujah, and great balls of fire! I love Jesus and I feel good! I feel good, good, *good!*"

Overflowing with the spirit, Jimmy Divine stuttersteps across the stage.

"You know, Brothers and Sisters, mine has always been a wayfarin' ministry. I travel the length and breadth of this great Christian land of ours, goin' where the good Lord wills. And when He said, 'Brother Jimmy, I want you to do your next show live from Puerto Rico,' I fell to my knees and cried out, 'Thank you, Jesus!' Because this lovely little Caribbean island may be small in size, but it is majestic in its myriad blessings. If you like your ocean blue and your beaches golden, if you like your weather sunny and your neighbors warm, friendly, and unswervingly Christian, then, my friends, you will find our fifty-second state is truly a little piece of God's Own Heaven on Earth!"

Jimmy Divine may be bending the truth a little about those beaches golden and that ocean blue—outside of the protected stretches of coastline reserved for the pleasure of high church folk and tourists only, they do not exist—but the hometown crowd eats that stuff up. They rock the place with amens and hallelujahs, cheering and stomping.

Jimmy Divine raises a hand for silence.

"Friends, we have a really big show in store for you. And as a special treat, later on in the evenin' we will be choppin' off the hands of six convicted thieves, live, right here on *It's Jimmy Divine Time!*"

The studio audience goes nuts. Jimmy Divine puts on a Devil of a show. Now, he leans toward us confidingly, as though he is letting us in on some very hush-hush dope.

"I kind of loosed the cat outta the bag there about what we're plannin' for those thieves, 'cause I want you to gather the kiddies around the viddy screen so's they can witness the wages of sin firsthand."

The crowd yells, "Bless the children!"

"Of course, we got the finest microsurgeons in the world standin' by backstage to sew them hands back on—Christians know how to forgive—but there's an important lesson to be learned here just the same."

The crowd yells, "Praise the Lord!"

"But before we get to that exaltin' moment of divine retribution, won't you please give a listen to these important words?"

Image splash!

A mountain road. An ominous gray sky.

Image splash!

A 2099 Miracle Gran Turismo whips through curves and dips, hugging the highway.

"Brother or Sister," Brother Conn Darden intones, "whether your car runs on hydrogen, solar power, or evil-smelling, old-fashioned methane, you want every road you drive to be a highway to Heaven."

The Miracle's front tire eats up the road.

Image splash!

Lightning flashes. Thunder crashes. A heavy squall lashes the landscape. The tire throws up a rooster tail of spray.

Image splash!

That famous figurine we all know and honor, the belovèd Plastic Jesus of legend and century-old tradition, materializes above the car's dashboard. The statuette fills the giant screen. Jesus' hinged right hand swings up and down, doling out blessings with each dip in the road.

Image splash!

The driver smiles. The Brother has beautiful teeth. And he is clearly enjoying the easy handling of his powerful new automobile, along with the security of having his Redeemer riding shotgun for him.

Image splash!

A Plastic Mary materializes on the dashboard of a different car. The Mary's hands are clasped together, and her hinged head bobs in prayer with the car's motion.

Smiling sweetly, a pure young blonde Sister pilots the Virgin's car, a sleek, powerful Silver Seraphim SupR/Turbo XT.

Image splash!

The two muscle cars whip around a slick rain-drenched curve and—

Oh, no! Oh, no!

PANIC!

The Brother tromps down on his brake pedal.

The Sister stomps hers with both feet.

Extruded nu-silk radials shriek. Nano-assisted suspension systems stagger.

The Gran Turismo spins out of control.

The SupR/Turbo skids broadside.

Terrified blue eyes. Screaming white teeth.

in ultra slow motion
the cars
kiss
collapse
crumple
¡EXPLODE! ¡EXPLODE!
¡EXPLODE!
like
fiery
hellflowers
blossoming

"Yes, friends," Brother Conn intones, as a choir begins humming softly in the background, "you can never know what twist of fate may lie in wait just around the next bend. So wherever *you* travel, take along the brand-spanking-new Traditional Plastic Jesus or the totally redesigned improved Classic Plastic Mary, and assure yourself that, no matter what happens, little old Y-O-U won't be going to H-E-double-L."

Image splash!

The fireball freezes.

Enveloped in shimmering pastel halos, the Plastic Jesus and the Plastic Mary materialize on either side of the fireball to a sweet a cappella chord from the choir.

"These handsome examples of nonbiodegradable, one-hundred-percent American Christian art are made of genuine, antique superpolystyrene, guaranteed to last from here to eternity."

A phone number flashes onscreen. Viewers should order *now*. Friendly, courteous, helpful operators are standing by. The choir underlines the invitation with a chorus of seductive a cappella "Oohs."

"Either one—or both—can be yours absolutely free, by simply sending your voluntary contribution of two hundred fifty, five hundred, or one thousand dollars—or more, if you *really* want to do right by Jesus—to cover shipping and handling. Donations from overseas: five percent extra."

The choir erupts in bouncy four-part harmony:

> *I really wanna do right by Jesus!*
> *Wanna do right, even if it's hard!*
> *Really wanna do right by my Jesus!*
> *Sweet Jesus, charge my card!*

Cristo, that is a good commercial.

Even though it is going to sop up the little credit I have left to cover what remains of the month—Angela and I will not be treating ourselves to a sushi feast at Número Tres for at least ten days—I really do want to do right by Jesus. That is why I am going for the set: a brand-spanking-new Traditional Plastic Jesus for this humble servant and a totally redesigned improved Classic Plastic Mary for Angela.

The way I see it, number one: I am contributing to help further the Lord's work on earth. And, number two: I am investing in Salvation.

It is the best of all possible purchases.

Sweet Jesus, charge my card!

3∅

In a helojet, you can climb above the smog and see the sky that God intended—clear, clean, blue, and bright, like a coat of shiny enamel. I never imagined the world could look this lovely. Sure, I have seen such sights on the viddy, but live and in person is something else. The clouds gleam. The air is as clear as God's Mind. Far below, though, smog blankets the Island like a shroud.

"Ever flown before?" Jimmy Divine asks, whipping the helo through a counterclockwise arc.

"No, sir."

I half smile, half grimace at the sinking sensation in my stomach. Whoo-eee! This is fun, the best joyride ever. "I guess maybe this is how God sees the world, huh?" I say.

"You think so?"

"Well, I can't actually *know*, of course." I shrug. "But if He does see it like we're viewing it now, I don't suppose He's very happy with what we've done to it."

Jimmy Divine grins. "What's wrong with what folks have done to it?"

We fly east. The grease smudge that is the neighboring island of St. Thomas stains the horizon a hundred miles dead ahead. The mucky blob of Puerto Rico looms just to our right. Directly below, the ocean sparkles deepwater blue. But instead of blending into clear lime or turquoise as it rolls shoreward, the Atlantic turns sludgy brown.

"Just look at the unspoiled beauty up here, and look at what we've done down there," I say.

"Maybe God wants it that way," Jimmy Divine says. "Ever consider that?"

The thought had never entered my mind.

"Why would He want it that way? It was supposed to be Eden. That's what He intended for Adam and Eve and their descendants."

I shiver. I did not expect to be this cold up here, and nobody thought to suggest that I wear anything warmer than my usual tropical-issue jumpsuit.

"But humankind is weak, boy. You should know that by now. They screwed up something fierce barely outta the box, and got themselves booted. Been slidin' downhill ever since. Last hundred years or so, they really been gainin' speed."

Jimmy Divine powerswoops so we are barely skimming

the waves. My heart pounds. My blood tingles. The ocean stretches ahead like the broadest of highways—one with no need for penance lanes—and the whitecaps rocketing by beneath us look like blurred lane markers.

"Anyway," Jimmy Divine continues, "wasn't it the Lord Hisself said go multiply and fill the earth?"

"But when are we supposed to stop multiplying?"

Jimmy Divine laughs. "He didn't rightly say, did He?"

"Seems to me we filled the earth some time ago, and we've been mucking it up ever since."

We zip along, devouring space. My forearms ache from my grip on the armrests.

"Maybe that's the whole point," Jimmy Divine says. "Maybe folks are supposed to keep muckin' it up. Maybe Adam and Eve's original sin was so terrible, God wanted a punishment big enough to fit the crime. Maybe His idea was, since humans saw fit to trash the gift of Paradise, He'd just set them loose to turn their dumb little planet into a living Purgatory. Or, if they were stupid and nasty enough, to make it into a regular Hell on Earth, get the kind of world they deserved. If things ain't already there, boy, they sure are getting blessèd close, dontcha think?"

What I do not like about Jimmy Divine's theory is that it makes a kind of horrible sense. Nor do I like the note of glee in the way he tells it.

"It's kinda nice to be able to talk to you about such things, boy—you know, father to son."

He gives me a comradely wink.

"You just might turn out to be a chip off the ol' block after all."

I get a wonderfully warm feeling inside. Then we hit a pocket of turbulence that makes my stomach do flipflops.

31

Cristo, those are the ruins of Fort San Felipe del Morro looming ahead! I recognize the watchtower and the domed sentry boxes. Why is Fabiola piloting us into this off-limits area? Even our newly installed Plastic Jesus seems to be bobbing warily on the dashboard. And why is she driving so slowly? Should I ask, or should I try keeping my trap shut for a change?

What would Fabiola do if our positions were reversed? It does not take long to figure out the answer to that question—she would hold her tongue and see what develops. So that is what I will do.

Six centuries ago, the Spanish began erecting these thick battlements that sweep up from the sea a hundred meters or more. They took almost three hundred years to complete. The ancient fortress that held the English and the Dutch at bay more than once is a huge dark presence against the moon-washed sky. As we bounce over the buckled surface of the abandoned access road, a news-breaker reports on the dashboard viddy:

"Twelve million cheering Chinese turned out to greet newly elected Pope Pius the Thirteenth—the former Yao Cardinal Hongwen—upon his visit to Beijing's Tiananmen Square on the first leg of the rookie pontiff's so-called Victory Tour. Pius the Thirteenth is the Christian Catholic Church's first pope of Chinese descent.

"Brazilian Mars colony Ribeira Preta remains under the control of New Christer insurgents. Attempts to dislodge the rebels have so far proved fruitless. But a government spokescleric says, 'A camel has a better chance of passing through the eye of a needle than these heretics have of overcoming the minions of the Lord.'

"And as the world moves ever closer to its Final Days, the nationwide manhunt for the Twin Antichrists continues.

"This is Rosanna Marie Marchán, Christian American Capsule News Network."

Fabiola parks beneath a palm tree. She stares at the midnight shape of the fort.

"What are we doing here, Muñoz?" I blurt out.

Drat! I just could not hold it in, could I? I could kick myself. I will never become like Fabiola.

"You know the desperate kind of people who live in these ruins," I say. Fabiola says nothing. "Why are you acting so blessèd mysterious?"

She does not look her usual confident, contained self. Her face is tight, her lips dry.

"You want to meet the Children, don't you?" Her voice sounds huskier than usual.

"Meet what children?" ¡Dios mío! Michael Moron. "You mean the Twin Messiahs?"

"You've been so Cathy Curious about them, I thought maybe you should get the chance to meet them."

"Tonight? Here?"

I cannot believe it. I have done it! This is the break-through Jimmy Divine and the archbishop have been pressuring me for. Fat little Tony Malpica would throw cartwheels if he knew. Jimmy Divine would be grinning like the Devil.

But there is no joy in my heart. I feel like somebody just kicked me in the gut.

I am not ready for this. I know I am supposed to be seeking the Twin Redeemers, but I never thought I would actually find them.

The authorities have tacitly ceded these abandoned ruins to the homeless and the lawless. Tales of violence and mayhem run rampant, and it is said that even Avenging Angels dare not enter at less than squad strength.

"The Twins are *here*, where even Avenging Angels fear to tread?" I ask, trying to keep the shakiness out of my voice.

"The Twins are everywhere."

What is that supposed to mean?

"Come on," Fabiola says.

We get out of the van.

The sharp odors of earth and salt spray assault us. We

snake through groves of palm trees, bull through waist-high weeds. Sawgrass snags on my jumpsuit. Shadow and moonlight dapple our faces.

Our boot heels clack loudly as we cross the ancient stone bridge that spans the moat. Where a water-filled ditch once prevented attacking soldiers from reaching the gates of the fortress, wild growth now waits to swallow whole the unwary.

The surf booms. The wind whistles and moans. Palm leaves scraping against one another creak like unoiled doors. In daylight, these noises mean nothing. In the dead of night, they turn strange and threatening.

My nerves feel raw. My skin crawls.

Huge wooden gates set into the mottled walls of the fort loom up ahead. Fabiola raps on them in code.

No answer.

My ears buzz. My heart pounds.

Fabiola gestures patience. Minutes drag by.

Despite the warm December night, a shiver runs down my spine. What is taking so blessèd long? I have a bad feeling about this.

Does Fabiola suspect that I am acting under instructions from the Shepherdess herself? Received indirectly, by way of the Shepherdess's instruments, the archbishop and Jimmy Divine, of course, but still, from the Shepherdess. Am I walking into a trap?

Although I cannot imagine why Fabiola would suspect me of anything. I am just a rookie soulsaver, fresh out of training and still wet behind the ears. That is the image of me I believe she sees, and I do not think I have done anything to prompt her to change it.

Suddenly, locks rattle, deadbolts squeal, rusty hinges squeak. The gates creak ajar.

Fabiola slips through them, pulls me in after her.

The gates close behind us. Deadbolts slam home. I swallow hard. A moment ago, we were locked out. Now we are locked in.

I venture down a wide alleyway that leads into a stone courtyard ringed by ancient blockhouses, their facades punctuated by dark doorways. Two steep stone ramps slope up to higher levels. Ahead, a third ramp dives into an arched tunnel.

Fabiola catches up. I notice a figure shambling after us, a torch guttering in one enormous hand. It is the Brother who manned the gates, a hulking giant in a patched robe with the hood up, padding silently in our wake. Fabiola turns to him. He raises his free hand, fingers forming a **V**. Fabiola mirrors the gesture.

"Hola, Cristóbal," she says.

Behind Cristóbal, clumps of people dressed in rags are cooking scraps over makeshift fires. They eye us warily.

A mongrel with a lot of Irish wolfhound in it bursts into furious barking. Wild-eyed, it races to intercept us, snarling and flashing yellow teeth and silvery strings of muzzle slime.

Its nails scrabble on stone. The monster tenses to spring. My knees go weak.

"Hush, Pentecost," Cristóbal growls.

The dog freezes, its massive head level with my chest, every muscle taut. It growls deep in its throat, weaving its muzzle in a frustrated figure 8. Its sour breath engulfs me.

But it is under control, and if I am to do my duty by the archbishop, I must be able to identify these people later. I sidle as close as I can to Cristóbal and try to sneak a look at his face, under the hood.

The gatekeeper sees my intention. He throws back his cowl and thrusts his scarred, one-eyed face into mine.

I stumble back. Pentecost growls.

Cristóbal glares at me with his good eye. He looks sickening. Why not just have a new eye grown?

I expect him to challenge me. Instead, he jerks his thumb over his shoulder and says, "Better hurry, or you'll lose her, Brother."

Relieved, I scurry away. Pentecost lurches after me, but Cristóbal whacks his rump. The dog whimpers and sits.

Fabiola vanishes through a portal across the courtyard. I rush in after her. The room is pitch-dark. I trip over a tilted flagstone, twist my ankle, and hit the floor hard, scraping my palms and bruising some ribs. I grunt at the pain.

I can just make out Fabiola, dimly outlined by reflected moonlight, though I can distinguish nothing else, not even the walls.

Coded tapping on thick wood. A barred door creaks open.

"Fabiola . . . ?" I whisper, afraid of being left alone in the dark with no place to go except back to Cristóbal and his hellhound.

A section of wall slides back, framing a figure robed and cowled, carrying a torch. A woman. She offers Cristóbal's two-fingered greeting. Fabiola returns the sign of the **V**. The woman nods and retreats down a tunnel.

Fabiola gestures for me to go ahead of her.

I do, reluctantly. Following, she stops only to slide the wall shut behind us. The sound of the crossbar dropping back into place echoes down the passageway. There is no going back now.

The tunnel narrows. We advance in single file. The woman with the torch is a dim form ahead. The air grows dank, oppressive. I tiptoe, afraid to make noise.

"What is this place?" I whisper to Fabiola.

"Secret underground passageways the Spaniards built way back when to connect the fortifications of the Old City. In case of siege."

I make the **V** sign. "What is this?"

"The Sign of the Twins."

Our guide turns a corner. The tunnel dims sharply.

"Can we hurry?" I mutter. "I don't like the dark."

I hustle to catch up, on tiptoe. I must look like a demented ballet dancer.

We round the corner. Tall striped candles flicker, illuminating an underground chapel with a small marble altar and dark wooden pews. The room smells musty. Shadows dance everywhere. Niches in the rock walls house wooden carvings of Saint Anthony, Saint Francis, Saint Theresa, and Our Lady of the Sorrows, all stained with age.

Our guide gestures for us to wait, and disappears through a door behind the altar. I settle into a back pew next to Fabiola, sliding close enough to feel the comforting heft of her hip against mine.

I look up. Two children stand before the altar. They are the same height, and both seem to be about twelve years old. Thick black hair frames strong Latino features and gentle, yet penetrating, almond eyes. The boy takes the girl's hand. They smile at me, and those marvelous eyes fill with warmth. Never have I seen children so beautiful.

"These are the Children of God, Juan Bautista," Fabiola says. "And this is their mother, María de Dios."

Our guide lowers her cowl, revealing thick, straight black hair, watchful eyes, delicate Hispanic features.

On second glance, I realize that the Twins are no handsomer than many other children. But these two project—I do not know exactly how to describe it—a sense of power and self-containment I have never felt before, not even from the Shepherdess herself.

"I . . . wanted to meet you," I manage.

They smile again. The candlelight casts confusing shadows around them.

"We know," the boy says. "We know you, Juan Bautista."

"We are glad you came," the girl says, "because we want you to know us."

Under Fabiola's watchful eye, we begin to speak.

32

Morning light outlines Angela's gentle features. I sit at the foot of our bed, still wearing my rumpled uniform. It amazes me how my heart swells with the urge to keep her safe from any harm. How did someone I did not even know six months ago entwine her soul with mine so quickly and completely? What did I ever do to deserve such a blessing?

Angela's eyelids open drowsily. "Juan Bautista . . . ?"

She takes in my red-rimmed eyes, overnight stubble, and haggard face, and instantly sits up. The hem of her marriage robe rides up on her thighs.

"What's the matter, Juan Bautista?"

I do not know where to start. She slides across the bed, cradles me in her arms, strokes my face and hair. I feel protected, cared for, safe.

"Have you been up all night?" she asks.

"I couldn't sleep."

"What's wrong?"

I don't know what to say. "Too much on my mind."

"Tell me." It is both an invitation and a plea.

I pause far too long, then say, "I can't."

Something behind her eyes flinches. "I'm your wife," she tells me.

She speaks softly, but with suddenly fierce eyes. I feel like a heel, yet I am enormously proud of her. It is a blessing to be held in the heart of another. I am filled with gratitude and wonder that she could care so much for me when I feel so utterly unworthy of her.

I look at her, searching for—what? Understanding? Comfort? Compassion? My eyes feel sandpapery from exhaustion. I would give anything to sleep, but too many questions gnaw at me.

"I love you," Angela says. "You can tell me anything."

For better or for worse, we vowed. *For better or for worse.* I ponder the meaning in those words, and for the first time I understand that I truly *can* tell her anything, that she is willing to share the burden I have been trying to shoulder alone.

How heartbreakingly strange that we should have to plead with the people who most need our help to let us help them. But there it is. Even now, I speak without looking at her, as though I am ashamed.

"I've seen them," I tell her.

"Seen whom?"

"The Christ Children. I spoke with them."

Angela's eyes widen. Surely this was the last thing she expected to hear from my lips.

"The Twin Redeemers are *here*, in Puerto Rico?" she asks softly.

Is she shocked? Frightened? Appalled?

"And you spoke with them?" she says carefully.

I nod.

"Alone?"

I nod again.

"What did they say?"

The question takes me by surprise. Why this unexpected interest in the Children's words? Surely the first concern of a good Christian should be for the capture of the Children, not what they said. The night we put aside our marriage robes, I glimpsed an aspect of Angela I never imagined existed, but now it occurs to me that she may be even more complicated.

"What did they say, Juan Bautista?"

There was so much that we spoke of, or that I wished we had spoken of, in the catacombs beneath El Morro. But no specific words come to mind, just a *sense* of what they wanted me to understand.

"They said . . . that we are supposed to love one another. And help one another. That we are supposed to do what we know is right, even when it is hard—*especially* when it is hard."

I remember the ideas, the concepts. They were majestic. Vaulting. Compelling. They filled my heart to bursting, yet I cannot give them voice. My words are too pale to do them justice.

Angela's brow furrows, as though she had expected... *more*.

"But everybody knows that," she says. "It's in the Catecismo."

"That's what *I* said."

"What did *they* say?"

I take a deep breath, think back. I try to recapture the glow of what they told me. "They said everybody knows it, but too few live it. They said we are so busy being holy, we have forgotten to be good."

My words sound trite, hokey. It is very frustrating.

"¿Y tú, Juan? Do you believe in them?" Angela asks.

When I was with the Children, everything seemed clear. On my own, it is all murky.

I shake my head. "I don't know what I believe anymore."

Angela considers. "Son profetas falsos. That's what the Shepherdess calls them."

It is not exactly an accusation. More like... a test. To see how I will handle it.

"I know," I say, and go her one better. "The Shepherdess says they are the Antichrists."

Angela considers again. "Maybe you're being sucked in," she says slowly.

The thought is scary. I am indeed lurching about on swampy ground that could swallow me whole. At any moment, I could stumble into a patch of quicksand and disappear.

Maybe I am already sinking.

"But when you talk to them," I say, "you feel in your bones that every word they speak is the truth."

Maybe I should not be in a rush to inform the archbishop. Maybe I should take the time to think things through.

"They say the Devil is a smooth liar," Angela says.

"That's what worries me," I reply. "Somebody is lying to me, Angela, and I'm not sure who it is."

33

We are seated in our pews, looking at the wrong end of a Sunday shift, and already I am bone tired from lack of sleep and wrestling with my private demons.

"—and guide us with Your infinite love and wisdom," Father Emilio concludes, "for it is Your holy work that we humbly try to do. Amen."

"Amen," we chorus.

The squad is at full strength, except for Fabiola, who is late for noon roll call. She must have overslept after our all-nighter.

I am a little concerned about Angela. After we spoke earlier this morning, she suddenly got nauseous and barely made it to the bathroom before she threw up. Not that she had much to get rid of. We had not eaten breakfast yet. She told me it was a normal side effect of being pregnant. The doctors even have a name for it, morning sickness. She thought something she ate might have disagreed with the baby, maybe the yellowtail she had in the dorm mess hall last night was a little off. She said it was nothing serious. Besides, she has always had a weak stomach. Seeing somebody Billy Barf like that kills my appetite, though, so my last nourishment was yesterday's shish kebab with Fabiola before the visit to El Morro. Now my stomach is growling, and I feel a little light-headed.

On the plus side, it is a day in a million. Nearly blue sky, practically white clouds, almost clear air. Across the bay, the statue of Christopher Columbus glistens in the blurry sun. Traffic on the Morro Bridge nearby flows like molasses. One good thing about Sunday shifts: folks are in church if it is morning, at the beach if it is afternoon—or home if it is raining—so the surface roads are clearer to roll on.

Father Emilio wraps it up. "All right, people, let's go out there and save some souls."

We sidestep out of our narrow pews and head for the vans in bay 1, me chatting and joking with Luis Zambrana, Nelly Rivera, and the others. Father Emilio beckons to me. I excuse myself and return, apprehension clumping up in my belly. Why would Father Emilio want to speak with me today of all days?

"You wanted to see me, Father?" I say brightly, trying to hide my exhaustion.

"Where is your partner, son?"

That is the question I feared he was going to ask. "I don't know, Father," I say, favoring him with my most puzzled look. "Maybe she overslept. We pulled a late shift last night."

Not exactly true. Okay, a blatant lie. But I cannot say my partner is late because we stayed up all night chatting with the objects of the most intensive manhunt in the nation's history, now can I?

Father Emilio accesses the duty roster. "Your van isn't checked in either."

This surprises me. "That's odd," I blurt out.

Father Emilio glances up from the terminal screen. "Why is that?"

Oops! How can I explain without giving myself away? To throw off any suspicions I may have raised in Father Emilio, I decide to admit to a lesser offense.

"Fabiola and I," I say, putting on an air of guilty apology, "well, we ran a little late last night, so to save me the trip here and back, I debriefed on the van's brain and Fabiola dropped me off at my dorm. She was supposed to bring the van in."

"What time was that?"

"Three, maybe four."

"In the morning?"

I nod. Father Emilio checks his terminal.

"Didn't you pull the six-to-twelve?"

"Yeah, we did, we did. But we got to shooting the Bobby Bull after." I shrug, throw up my hands helplessly, grin—one of those has got to work. "You know how it is."

One of them does. Father Emilio beams.

"Sure," he says, nodding in a comradely fashion. "It hasn't been so long since I was out soulsaving, too, you know. Maybe Fabiola decided to hang on to the van and bring it in this morning. I used to do that myself from time to time, but don't tell anybody." He checks his terminal. "Hmm. She hasn't called in sick, and her pager is dead."

This is very odd. "It isn't like Fabiola not to show up," I say.

Father Emilio looks concerned. "I'll have to put a trace on your meat wagon."

"What should I do in the meantime?"

Father Emilio looks around. We are alone. He seems to come to a decision.

"Tell you what, Lorca." He places a fatherly hand on my shoulder. "I've got six teams set to roll, Sundays are always slow, and I can't send you out without a van and a partner anyway, so why don't you take the day off and get some rest? You look beat, boy."

"Are you sure?" I say.

Father Emilio nods.

"Thanks. I could use the naptime."

And the chance to discuss my misgivings with Angela some more. Because I sure feel the need.

I head for my cubicle to check my mailbox. My toe and heel caps click on the ceramic floor tiles. The place is empty, everyone out on patrol. I thumb my terminal screen and say, "Mail Call. Lorca." Bright red letters fill the screen.

CONFIDENCIAL/CONFIDENTIAL
FAVOR INDICAR CÓDIGO DE ACCESO/
PLEASE INPUT ACCESS CODE

I code in my password. A message appears in English, my default language on the office brain. Seven heart-stopping letters.

CONFESS

My heart races. I gulp air.

Who sent this? And why?

I have to stay sharp, think straight, get my thoughts organized. But my head feels like it is stuffed with cotton.

Deep breath . . . calm down . . . okay . . .

All right. Now, review the facts. Slowly.

The only person who knows I have seen the Christ Children is Angela.

Well, and Fabiola.

Oh, and the Children themselves. And their mother. And Cristóbal the gatekeeper. And—

Cristo, it is a blessèd mob!

Still, none of them would have any reason to tell anybody.

But what if the archbishop has somebody watching me?

My blood chills.

That is nuts, Lorca. Malpica would not do that. *You* are spying for *him*. One does not spy on one's own spies.

Unless one does not trust them.

Why would he not trust me? I am Jimmy Divine's son. He knows that.

But what if Malpica has found out that I have seen the Children and have not reported it to him?

I need to know who sent this. I need to know who—

Cristo, where are my brains? That data gets logged in for every message. Problem solved.

"Sender?" I ask.

Bright red letters fill the screen:

NO RECORD

No record?! There *must* be a record. There is *always* a record. Records are an integral part of the system.

But the system is not infallible. I suddenly remember how my first jumper found a way to beat the system by scattering his brains over ten square meters of ledge.

Uh-oh.

Okay, back to square 1. Who sent the message? More important, why?

The click of approaching toe and heel caps plunges me into serious panic. Who could that be? My squadmates are all out on patrol. I thought I was alone here. I glance over my shoulder—

—and breathe again. It is Father Emilio.

I tap the screen. The messages vanish, to be replaced by an inquiry.

[SAVE] [DELETE] MESSAGE?

Quickly, I tap [DELETE], take a deep breath, and turn toward Father Emilio. I am slick with fear sweat.

"Something wrong, Lorca?"

I can brazen this out. "No, Father," I say. My body shivers. "Why?"

"You don't look well, son. Very pale." Father Emilio's brow wrinkles. "You're drenched in perspiration. And you're shivering. Are you running a fever?"

He places his hand on my forehead. It feels soft and warm, like I imagine my mother's hand must have felt when she was still alive and caring for her firstborn and only baby boy.

"Hmm . . . no fever," Father Emilio says. "In fact, a little on the cool side. Perhaps you should see a healer."

I am a little dizzy. "I don't think it's physical, Father." I should eat, get some sleep.

"Ah." Father Emilio looks at me thoughtfully, purses his lips. "Well, in that case, maybe your confessor."

"My . . . confessor?"

CONFESS.

My blood chills. Awash in paranoia, I search Father Emilio's face. Did he intend some hidden meaning?

The squad padre shrugs. "He is not there merely to forgive us our trespasses, you know."

He digs an elbow into my sore ribs, and gives me a broad wink.

I mask the pain and squeeze out a smile.

My stomach growls.

34

I stumble into a slidewalk confessional and log on. Instead of Father René, I get the Digital Jesus.

"B-B-Bless you, my child," He says. "All our l-l-l-lines are b-busy, but your p-p-p-priest will be with you before you can say 'The Power and the G-G-Glory.'"

Wonderful.

The electronic Redeemer melts into a misty shot of the Shepherdess. She strolls through a woodsy nook overflowing with roses, orchids, and gillyflowers. She looks pure and radiant. Her dewy lips and sleepy eyes make my heart thump.

She sings.

Jesus loves me, this I know,
For the Bible tells me so.

Normally, I could listen to her sweet voice forever. But today I am so nervous, I am jogging in place on my knees.

The flawless face of the Shepherdess dissolves into Father René's pockmarked one. I jump right in.

"Father, I found a strange message in my mailbox—"

He jumps in at the same time. "I'm sorry I had to be so mysterious, but—"

Too concerned with my own worries to register what he is saying, I plunge ahead.

"Father, I'm Connie Confused. I don't know if what I have done is a sin and—"

I break off, afraid to speak the thing aloud, then decide just to blurt it out. I take a deep breath.

"I have met with the Christ Children, Father."

Father René nods urgently. "I know, my son—"

I know, my son? Whoa, folks. I am, to say the least, astonished. A million questions pop into my head, but only the dumbest one gets out.

"You do?"

"But it will have to wait. I have terrible news."

Oh, my Lord. I was right. The archbishop *knows.*

What will he do to me for not having gone to him? And why did I not? It is not like me to question authority or to disobey my elders.

But...the Children are smooth talkers. They cast a spell on me. Fabiola is right, I *am* malleable, too much so, and now I have got myself in way over my head, and I am going to have to pay.

"What do you mean?" I stammer.

"Fabiola is dead."

"What? Fabiola?!"

He speaks softly, but with great intensity. "Self-inflicted death, according to the report."

"Suicide? *Fabiola?* She had no reason."

"Of course not." Father René leans back. The move away from the wide-angle camera lens makes him seem to shrink. "But a band of Avenging Angels found her in the back of your van last night. Frozen. Their report says she had programmed the van to freeze her twice."

Twice? Oh, no!

Father René's eyes look bleak. "They notified me because I am her confessor of record." He leans forward. The move toward the lens distorts his face. "They have her body at San Francisco de Asís," he says. "Only I don't understand why, if she's frozen, they don't just revive her."

I do.

"Because refreezing is the first thing they teach you *not* to do in Corps training," I say. "Refreeze a thawed body, Father, and what you've got is a load of spoiled meat."

I learned that in my first week of *Fundamentals of Cryonics.* Refreezing crystallizes the fluids not just inside the body but also inside every microscopic bit of organ tissue, and that is like taking a million tiny knives and hacking up the interior of every cell. Crystallized meat is dead for keeps. Cathy Corpse.

"Poor, brave Fabiola," Father René whispers. "They murdered her."

Things are bad enough as it is. I do not need this extra twist. "Who murdered her, Father?"

His eyes get bleaker. "Those thugs who say they found her dead."

Why does he keep hitting me with new stuff when I am already so far off balance?

"The Avenging Angels?" I ask. Surely he is not referring to the Shepherdess's personal guardians.

Father René's voice is a whisper enveloping rage. "There is nothing angelic about the dirty work those goons do for the Shepherdess," he tells me.

My heart beats wildly. My head is splitting. I suck deep breaths, massage my temples with my fingertips. I cannot believe where this conversation has taken us. I came here wanting to hear someone say that my anxieties are nothing more than paranoid fantasies, not to be told . . . this.

I lean in close to the monitor screen. "Do you realize what you're saying?" I barely whisper.

Cristo, the *look* on Father René's face. Anger? Frustration? Pity?

"Understand something, Juan Bautista," he says in a barely controlled voice. "The Shepherdess wants the Twins badly. Somehow the Angels found out that Fabiola knew the Children's hiding place. And when she refused to betray the Twins, the Angels killed her, as a message to you."

Horror and disbelief must be writ large on my face, because Father René's voice fills with compassion. "There are evils of which you are still innocent, my son," he says.

I read a mixture of emotions in his face. It is the same mixture I saw in the mirror when I was trying to tell Angela about the Christ Children.

"What do you mean, a message to me?" I do not care for the sound of that.

"You are her partner. They think you know what she knew."

I grope for the words to express what should be self-evident. "But . . . I don't."

Father René's eyes narrow. "Don't you?"

A cold stone settles in my belly. "Not everything."

"But *they* don't know that. And you *do* know the most important thing," he says. "You know where the Twins are."

Something clicks. "You're a New Christer, aren't you?" I speak with absolute assurance.

That stops him. Maybe I am starting to get the hang of seeing below the surface. Right now, I can see his brain working behind his eyes.

Father René gives me a calculating look. "If you mean do I believe that these children represent the Second Incarnation of Our Lord Jesus Christ," he says, "yes, then I'm a New Christer, Juan Bautista."

He leans toward me again. His face stretches across the screen.

"And I think you are one of us, too."

Indignation constricts my throat. Everybody keeps trying to drag me into a battle for which I never volunteered. It makes me angry and afraid. I try to sound noncommittal. "I don't know myself yet."

"Your thoughts still waver, but in your heart you are one of us already, Juan," Father René grins. His teeth are small and slightly yellow. "Fabiola knew that. That is why she and the Children put their trust in you."

What am I to do? Everyone wants something different from me—the archbishop, my father, Fabiola, the Christ Children, Father René, Angela. I am caught in the middle. It is tearing me up.

"You are all so much more certain about things than I am," I say. Where did that whiny kiddy voice come from? "Confused is what I am, Father. Real confused. I don't know *who* to believe."

"Then believe in yourself, Juan Bautista," Father René says. "Look into yourself and believe what you see there."

"Oh, sure, that is so easy for you to say—"

"—and so difficult for you to do. I know." He favors me with an apologetic smile. "But when you come down to it, Juan Bautista, the only one who can save your soul is you."

For what seems like forever, we regard each other in silence. His eyes seem to be asking for more than I can give. Finally, he lowers his gaze. After a moment of reflection, he blesses me. "Go in peace, my son."

My confessor vanishes.

"Wait, Father, what should I do?" I cry out, lost in the wilderness of my fears.

But Father René is gone, and I am face-to-face with the Digital Jesus.

"D-D-Do unto others as you would have them d-d-d-do unto you."

35

CENTRO DE RESURRECCIÓN SAN FRANCISCO DE ASÍS

PERSONAL AUTORIZADO SOLAMENTE

SAINT FRANCIS OF ASSISI RESURRECTION CENTER

AUTHORIZED PERSONNEL ONLY

I pretend that the sign's restriction does not apply to me. I stride confidently through the door into a long, well-lit corridor. And slam into an orderly in a light-blue uniform rushing a corpsicle on an air litter down the hallway.

"Gangway, Brother!" the orderly shouts.

I flatten myself against the wall, but still catch a jab from his elbow where I bruised my ribs last night at El Morro.

Massaging the ache, I follow him. In my uniform, even as grungy and ripe as it has become, I look like I have legitimate business here. Up ahead, the orderly backs in through a pair of swinging doors and pulls the litter behind him.

Could this be it? The doors are still swinging when I reach them.

SALA DE RESURRECCIÓN
RESURRECTION ROOM

Wrong place. Now what?

Though I have no idea where I am headed, I stride purposefully down another hall. Two surgeons approach, sanitary helmets thrown back, conversing loudly enough for me to overhear. The woman is worried that her little boy will get bumped from his high church crèche to a common kiddy center, which means he will not qualify for a top dorm like mine when he is older, and he will lose out on the best food, the best housing, and the best contacts. I had that same worry when I was a crèche kiddy, but I like to think God kept His Eye on me, and made sure I always managed to squeak through.

I step aside to let the médicos pass. Engrossed in their conversation, they pay me no mind. To my left, I discover another pair of swinging doors.

SALA DE CONGELADOS
FREEZE ROOM

Down the hallway, the surgeons enter the room where the orderly I collided with went. Up ahead, three male nurses in pink jumpsuits man the computers at a ward control station. One of them notices me and nods in greeting. I nod back, and he returns to inputting data on his terminal.

I enter a room with huge metal lockers lining three of the walls. Cristo, it is freezing in here. My breath condenses in thick clouds.

An orderly in a quilted yellow winter-issue jumpsuit looks up from her terminal. She has brown eyes and a scar over her left eyebrow. A lot of people keep imperfections that simple cosmetic surgery could fix, for mortification of the flesh. The ID on her uniform says RAMÍREZ, CECILIA. I wish I were wearing winter issue, too. My cheeks tingle from the cold, and I am starting to shiver.

"Bless you, Brother," she says. "You're a long way from the loading dock. Are you lost?"

"Bless you, Sister." I struggle to keep my teeth from chattering. "I came to see someone."

"Family?"

I shake my head. "Partner."

Her eyes register disbelief. "A soulsaver? Here?"

I cannot say, "My confessor claims the Shepherdess had her Angels kill her," so instead I quote from the Catecismo: "The Devil can trick the dove into the jaws of the wolf."

The orderly nods. "Judge not lest ye be judged," she quotes in agreement. "Your partner must have come in while I was off duty. Name, please?"

"Muñoz, Fabiola."

The orderly leads me to one of the lockers and thumbs a touchpad. The locker glides out, its electric motor barely audible over the whisper of the subzero refrigerating system.

I look into Fabiola's dead eyes.

Her face is rimed with frost, her features twisted in pain. A lump forms in my throat. I am so cold in my tropical issue that my teeth start to chatter. Even the anger that boils inside me is icy.

"Her infosheet says she's a refreeze," the orderly tells me.

"I know."

"Can't bring her back till the médicos solve that." The orderly shakes her head sadly. "Could be years." Ramírez, Cecilia, is trying to be sympathetic.

"Could be centuries," I say bitterly.

"You must have faith, Brother."

I am surprised that someone can still be so certain and sincere, using these worn-out words that I have heard a million times before.

You must have faith. The answer when there is no answer.

"You're right, Sister," I say, gritting my teeth to keep them still. "You must have faith."

36

"That is a serious accusation you're levelin', son," Jimmy Divine says.

He lolls in a marble Jacuzzi, hot water burbling around his sunburned neck. His chest and shoulders look white as grubs. The suite is huge, with black leather chairs, onyx tables, a giant viddy screen, and thick, heavy, white foam flooring. So much space and luxury for just one person makes you marvel, but someone as valuable to society and as close to God as Jimmy Divine deserves all this and more.

The steam from the Jacuzzi makes me sweat. I feel slimy and out of place.

"Are you telling me the Angels did *not* kill Fabiola?" I say.

Jimmy Divine smiles the smile of a man blessed with a ton of patience.

"It sounds," he says, enunciating with great care, "like

you're stringin' together a bunch of wild-ass stories you heard second- and third-hand, and jumpin' to some pretty wild-ass conclusions."

"I saw her body," I say. "How wild-ass is that?"

Jimmy Divine ducks underwater, comes up exhaling, hair pasted to his forehead. He pushes the dripping strands back. Nubby wet clumps stick out like goat horns.

He squints up at me. "But you didn't see anybody kill her, now did you?"

"Fabiola would never have killed herself."

"Whoa, there, son. We talkin' about the same person?" Jimmy Divine runs his fingers through his hair, slicks it back straight and smooth, revealing a high forehead. "That woman has got a lifelong record of emotional instability. First, she's a true believer who turns in her husband for anti-Christian activities, then she goes over to the Antichrists body and soul." He slaps the water with the palm of his hand for emphasis, splashing some on me. "Hell, boy, her own mother damn committed suicide not six months ago."

He says all this in a quiet, controlled voice. Only his eyes blaze. And I, who am supposed to have right on my side, am shrill and whiny.

"She told me they killed her mother and made it look like a suicide," I say. "Same with her husband."

Jimmy Divine's eyebrows shoot up. "*Who* killed her mother?" he asks. "*Who* killed her husband?"

I cannot answer either question. Fabiola never named names. But when she told her story, you knew who "they" were without the names. Now, though, I am stuck.

"I . . . don't know exactly," I finally mutter. I gesture weakly. "The authorities."

Jimmy Divine is starting to get irritated with me. There is disdain in his eyes and a sneer on his lips. "The authorities," he overenunciates. "Who exactly is that, boy? Your confessor? The archbishop? The Shepherdess?"

I feel cornered, like I did when I would get called on in Sunday school. I wind up giving the same humiliating answer I gave so often then.

"I don't know."

"The Devil is workin' overtime to trick you over to his side, boy," Jimmy Divine says. There is warning in his tone, and anger. "And it looks like he has damn near got you fooled. Maybe you don't comprende how big the stakes we're playin' for are, son. But I know just the person to make you understand."

"Who?" I ask.

"Sister Sarah!" he calls.

I am completely confused. "How is Sister Sarah going to make me understand anything?"

Jimmy Divine gives me a look normally reserved for the mentally impaired. "Ain't you got a lick of sense? I am talkin' about the Shepherdess, boy."

"The Shepherdess . . . ?"

A withering look. "You believe *her*, don't you?"

"Well, of course I do." I am offended. "What kind of question is that?"

Sister Sarah saunters in from the bedroom. A red silk robe clings to her lush body. Through the door, I see mirrored ceilings, gold wall fixtures, and a huge round bed in red lacquer with intricate black-and-gold trim and rumpled black satin sheets. Sinful opulence.

Sister Sarah smiles sleepily. "Bless you, Brother Juan."

"Bless you, Sister Sarah," I mumble automatically.

Something weird happens. For a moment, I seem to see my mother in Sister Sarah's place, red silk molding itself to her body. Then my mother's face is replaced by Angela's. Or maybe I am just confusing my mother's face with Angela's, they resemble each other so much. Before I can wonder if I am hallucinating from lack of sleep, the image vanishes. Sister Sarah yawns and stretches luxuriously.

"Can I be of service, Brother Jimmy?" she asks.

"Be obliged if you would get me Sister Lucille on the phone, darlin'."

Jimmy Divine sounds all business now. While Sister Sarah traipses to the phone, he lights a slim cigar. The smoke filters through his lips like incense from a censer.

"You're phoning the Shepherdess?" I ask.

I know Jimmy Divine and the Shepherdess orbit in the same high circles, but the idea of being able to log a call and expect her to pick up the receiver herself seems simply in-blessèd-credible to me. It raises my father a few notches in my estimation.

"She's been wantin' to meet you," Jimmy Divine says. The cigar tip glows orange. The air grows murky. I can make out the trademark charming good-ole-boy smile that has reclaimed his face, but only barely. "It appears to me this would be a good time for it."

"*She* wants to meet *me*?" It is beyond belief.

"Didn't I tell you the Lord had plans for you?"

"Sister Lucille online, Brother Jimmy," Sister Sarah announces.

I am dizzy. And scared. Things are moving too fast. I barge in to confront my father with a murder, and wind up about to meet face-to-face with the essence of the Lord's presence on earth? It is too much.

"And bless *you*, Sister Lucille. I got a young man I'd like you to meet, if you're free later this evenin'... That's the one... I'll ask him."

Jimmy Divine looks over at me. "Seven tonight okay? That's when we're recordin' my show."

I can only nod, like some tongue-tied jíbaro fresh from a coffee plantation in the mountains of Ciales.

"He'll be there... And bless *you*, Sister Lucille."

Jimmy Divine grins.

The muscles of my face do not respond. But I do not care if I resemble some hick hill farmer. I am in awe.

37

"—no doubt these are the Final Days which are spoken of in the Book of Apocalypse!"

Jimmy Divine prowls the stage. His face radiates sincerity. "I see guerrilla conflicts in América Latina, food wars on the Dark Continent, and a bloody revolution on our own back doorstep, South of the Border, down May-hee-coe way."

A woman shouts, "Deliver us, Lord!"

Jimmy Divine beams. "I see a war of secession among Japan's Indo-Asian satellites! I see man-made viruses laying waste to the Australozealand Confederation! And I see the imminent destruction of Israel in the Middle East!"

The woman waves her bony arms. "Deliver us! Deliver us, Lord!" She reminds me of a praying mantis.

"I see hurricanes in Hungary and earthquakes in Ethiopia! I see volcanoes in Venezuela and forest fires in Fiji! I see blizzards in Burundi and floods in French Guiana! I see pestilence in Pakistan and plagues in Peru! I see ice storms in Iraq and droughts in Dahomey! Everywhere I look, I see pain and fear! Everywhere I look, I see suffering and loss!"

"Deliver us! Deliver us! Deliver us, Lord!"

"Listen to me, my Brothers and Sisters! Hear my words!" Jimmy Divine implores. "These are the days of miracles and wonders that are foretold us in the prophecies of Apocalypse! These are the days of the Antichrists!"

The praying mantis cries out, "Lord, protect us!"

"And it saddens me that some of our weaker brethren have fallen prey to the Father of Lies and gone over to the ranks of the so-called New Christers!"

"Save them, Jesus!"

"But don't you be givin' up on them, you hear? Those lost sheep can be brought back into the One True Fold!"

"Pray for them, Lord!"

"And just to prove there ain't no ifs, ands, or buts about that, let's bring on Brother Bubba Watkins, who we've had flown down here special from his hometown of Chunchila, Alabama, so's you can witness a child of Man who, like the Prodigal Son, was *lost* to us but then, by the grace of God, *returned!*"

Cheers and stomping. From the back of the house, a skinny black teener sprints down the center aisle. As he runs, the skirt of his canary-and-chocolate robe flaps around his ankles. I expect him to get tangled up in it and trip, but he makes it safely down front to the main step unit, scampers up onto the stage, and embraces Jimmy Divine tearfully.

Jimmy Divine turns him to face the audience. "Witness for the Brethren, Brother Bubba!" Jimmy Divine cries.

Brother Bubba is so excited, he cannot keep himself from jumping up and down in place even as Jimmy Divine grips both his shoulders from behind.

"I'm here to tell y'all I betrayed the Lord!" the boy shouts in a girlish soprano.

Anguished voices call out, "No, child! No!"

Brother Bubba shakes his head earnestly. "I did, oh, I did!" His eyes well up. "I swallowed the lies of the Children of Satan and"—his voice cracks—"turned my back on Jesus!"

"Lord, deliver us!" the praying mantis screams as though a lance has been driven into her breast. "Jesus *loves* you, child!"

"But I was lucky, Brothers and Sisters," Brother Bubba calls out. "I was so lucky, 'cause my momma dragged me to see Brother Jimmy, and begged him to pray for me."

Brother Bubba looks at Jimmy Divine and punches a clenched fist at the heavens to show their solidarity. Jimmy Divine punches *both* his fists high to show *his* solidarity is even greater than was asked for.

"When that good and righteous man standing there prayed his heart out over me," Brother Bubba says, index finger waggling excitedly in Jimmy Divine's direction, "the Lord plumb knocked the scales from my eyes, and I finally seen them twin devils clearly that call themselves Emma and Noel."

We crouch on the edge of our seats. You could hear an angel dance on the head of a pin.

"And on their foreheads," Brother Bubba whispers, "right by their rough, scaly horns, I seen the number six-sixty-six, which the Good Book tells us is the Mark of the Beast!"

I know that cannot be true—I have seen the Children, stood as close to them as I am to the woman in the seat next to mine right now—but still my heart beats faster.

The crowd is enthralled. Their eyes shine.

Doubts begin to stalk me. Have I, perhaps, seen the Children only as they wanted me to see them? Have I, perhaps, let myself be bamboozled by appearances again? When will I ever learn?

I am struck with the force of a fist slugging you in the solar plexus by how Jimmy Divine beams upon Brother Bubba throughout the teener's recitation. Why has Brother Jimmy never looked at me like that? A dark rage seeps through me. I know I am guilty of the sins of Anger and Envy, so I send up a quick prayer requesting forgiveness. Of course it will do me no good, because I have yet to put the bitterness out of my heart.

From the way he is bouncing around the stage, bobbing his head and windmilling his arms, it is clear that Brother Bubba is building up to his big finale.

"And, sure as I'm standing here today, I knew then that I'd placed my soul inside the very *maw* of the Devil," Brother Bubba cries. "But the Lord was giving me one last chance to repent!"

"Repent, Brother, repent!" wails the praying mantis.

"So I come back to Brother Jimmy," Brother Bubba says. His voice has become quieter but more intense. He sounds utterly sincere. "Nobody had to drag me this time. This time I wanted to see Brother Jimmy, this time I wanted Brother Jimmy's help. And Brother Jimmy, he took one look at me, and said, Bubba, you flat got to tell everybody your story, because there is so many folks needs reminding that the Lord will forgive even the worst sinner if he but truly repents."

"Praise the Lord!"

"Ain't that an inspirin' story of salvation, Brothers and Sisters?" Jimmy Divine exults.

The faithful cheer. Jimmy Divine embraces the boy. The faithful appear transfigured. My face knots up in jealous anger. Instantly, I am ashamed, which only enrages me more.

"And now, to cleanse Brother Bubba's spirit and welcome our own prodigal son back into the shelter of God's bosom," Jimmy Divine says, "here is the person y'all been waitin' on. Our own belovèd Keeper of the Flock, Sister Alma Lucille Ferris!"

Glitter and tinsel cascade heavenward to reveal the figure of the Shepherdess. Baby spotlights frame her in a rose-tinted circle of light. She stands hip-deep in the waters of the Hark the Herald Angels Sing Portable Above Ground Baptismal Pool. The hem of her robe floats around her waist, and a faint smile dances on her lips.

Jimmy Divine escorts Brother Bubba to the pool. The stagehands must have forgotten to warm the water, because the boy shudders as he lurches in.

The Shepherdess opens her arms to the prodigal son. He fits himself into her embrace. She places one hand on his shoulder, the other on the crown of his head. "Child, in the name of our Lord, Jesus Christ," she intones in that clear musical voice, "I take you back into His bosom."

The Shepherdess pushes Brother Bubba under. To everyone's shock and surprise, he struggles. Kicking and thrashing, he drags her down with him. The crowd is thunderstruck. Seconds later, Brother Bubba and Sister Lucille burst gasping from beneath the holy waters. The Shepherdess's soaked vestments mold themselves to her body like Sister Sarah's red silk robe clings to the redhead's every curve. The chilly plunge has made the Shepherdess's nipples proud.

Brother Bubba bursts into tears. The Shepherdess clasps his head to her generous breast. The praying-mantis woman weeps in sympathy. The Shepherdess sings.

> *Amazing Grace, how sweet the sound*
> *That saved a wretch like me.*
> *I once was lost, but now am found*

38

Was blind, but now I see.

God gave her the voice of an angel, the face of a madonna, the loving heart of His own belovèd mother. The Shepherdess is so beautiful and sings so purely and with such aching sweetness that tears spring to my eyes.

I swipe at them with the back of my hand, while the Shepherdess refills our wineglasses. On the giant wall screen of the Presidential Suite, the image of the Shepherdess caresses that last crystalline note. The studio audience I was part of just an hour earlier bursts into cheers and applause.

I sip the wine, a dry Chilean red that must have cost a week's take of the collection plate.

On the wall screen, cameras pan the crowd.

There, gripping the front edge of the stage, is the

praying-mantis woman, tears streaming down her gaunt cheeks. There, to her left, is a pale teener, clapping his hands raw. There, several rows back, is a skinny Sister with a nine-month belly, triumphant arms in the air, swaying from side to side. There, standing on a chair, is a gaunt old man, pounding his sunken chest with a bony fist. There, stamping my feet, am I, fingers between my teeth to honor Our Lord with a piercing whistle. And there is the Shepherdess, water dripping from her hair and robe as she embraces Brother Bubba. Makes you proud to be a Christian.

The Shepherdess eases down next to me on the sofa and blanks the screen. She wears a white silk robe. I am still in my stinky SPCA jumpsuit.

"Don't turn it off!" I say. The words come out stronger than I had intended.

The Shepherdess pulls back a little, as though to observe me from a more comfortable distance. "Why not?" she says. "You were in the studio. You saw the whole session."

"It just seems more real on the viddy." I shrug helplessly, so silly does my explanation strike even me.

The Shepherdess wriggles into a more comfortable position next to me. "I thought maybe you and I could talk instead." She tops off our wineglasses. "You are performing a great service for the Church, Brother Juan, and I would like to get to know you better."

"Well, I...don't know what to say, except, I'm flattered...I guess, Sister...ahm." I stop, unsure how I should address her.

The Shepherdess smiles. "Go on."

I feel myself blushing. "Sister . . . Lu . . ."

My face is burning. The Shepherdess smooths out some wrinkles on the shoulder of my jumpsuit. "Go on, now," she says. Her voice sounds a little hoarse, maybe from the chilly water in the Hark the Herald Angels Sing Portable Above Ground Baptismal Pool.

I cannot. "It feels weird calling you Sister Lucille when you've always been the Shepherdess to me."

"But aren't we all Brothers and Sisters in Jesus and equals in the eyes of the Lord, Juan?"

"Of course we are." I strain and finally make it, "S-Sister Lucille."

Her eyes twinkle. "Again."

"Okay." Deep breath. "Sister Lucille." Like you would say, "Ball-peen hammer."

She leans closer. Her breath warms my cheek. "Say it like we're friends. I want us to be good friends."

The wine has misted up my eyes. The Shepherdess looks soft and blurry. Her skin seems to glow.

"Sister Lucille." I say it like we are old buddies.

"Sweet Brother Juan," she returns affectionately.

She treats me to a warm smile, and clinks her glass against mine. "¡Salud!" she says, and we drink, though to what I am not certain. Health, like she said, I guess. Friendship, maybe. Or to kindred souls. I am surprised at how comfortable I feel with her, at the sense of closeness, as though we share a spiritual bond. Maybe it has something to do with the fact that we have both been Chosen. Me in a much humbler role, of course. But still, you know, *Chosen.* It makes you feel validated.

We sit in silence. I am not used to being looked at the way the Shepherdess is looking at me. Searchingly. Intensely. It makes me nervous, so I try to rekindle the conversation. "I was going to say that I'm flattered, but I feel real Billy Bad."

"About what?" The Shepherdess sounds genuinely concerned.

"The . . . spying. The lying. The pretending to be something I'm not."

Her eyes widen with understanding. She clears her throat. "Of course you feel that way. You are a decent, Christian boy." She shifts her weight, and her breasts graze my arm. They feel warm, even through my jumpsuit. "But we are fighting a war, Juan Bautista, a holy war for the souls of our Sisters and Brothers. Each one who falls prey to the Antichrists is damning his or her soul for all eternity."

Her intensity is enthralling. Her nearness makes me tingle. Her lips look soft as pillows.

"We can't stand by and let that happen, can we?" she says huskily.

I shake my head. My throat feels dry. I swallow more wine. I feel like I am floating.

"We have to find those evil twins and stop them before it is too late," the Shepherdess whispers urgently. "But we are running out of time, and right now you are our best hope."

"Me?" My face feels numb.

"You, dearest Juan. You have been Chosen." Her smile is ardent. Her teeth are dazzling white. "The Lord told me to entrust myself to you, body and soul," she whispers. "Did you know that?"

She opens her arms. I freeze, terribly tempted to do something forbidden. Embarrassed, I turn away.

"Embrace me," she whispers. "It's all right."

I want to, but a part of me says it is wrong. The Shepherdess molds her body to mine, enfolds me in the hypnotic scent of gardenias. Her flesh is hot, her heavy-lidded eyes hypnotic. I feel stupid and clumsy.

"You are a beautiful, lovely boy, Juan Bautista," she whispers. "Kiss me."

Her mouth tastes like apples. Her tongue burns. Heat leaps from her flesh to mine. I can scarcely breathe.

"I'm . . . married," I manage to say.

Her lips move against mine. "It's all right," she murmurs. Her tongue traces my lips. "Mmm . . . you taste as sweet as the wine."

Our mouths melt into each other. Her lips and hands and body are sure and relaxed. Mine are nervous and awkward. But as our desire for one another mounts, my passion begins to equal hers.

"Sister Lucille . . . I . . . you're . . ."

"Hush, now, Juan," she murmurs, her mouth on mine. "Whatsoever you do for the Shepherdess . . . you do for her Sheep."

With a slow, confident hand, she unseals my jumpsuit.

Her fingers slip inside the fabric and begin stroking the tense muscles of my chest and belly.

"Oh, Juan Bautista," she whispers, "you are a sweet, pure boy."

Her hand slithers lower.

"Come minister to me, Juan, come minister to me."

39

I stumble back from the toilet. There are gold faucets in there, a gold showerhead, gold handles on the bidet. Gold in church is one thing. But in a room where you crap and pee and vomit?

The Shepherdess still sleeps, snoring lightly. The huge room is bathed in dim morning light that seeps in around the edges of the blackout curtains that cover the windows and the sliding doors to the balcony. My jumpsuit lies crumpled up on the floor, one wrinkled sleeve draped across the Shepherdess's robe.

Last night's glasses stand on the night table, their rims lip-smeared, their bottoms coated with gritty dregs of wine. Three empty bottles lie on their sides near the edge of the table. Wine stains speckle the white foam flooring below their uncorked mouths.

The Shepherdess breathes heavily and shifts her body, lifting a tangle of sheets to reveal a curve of leg, a hint of breast, a glimpse of face. It is hard to believe she is twice my age. Despite the ravages of wine, lovemaking, and sleep, she looks fabulous.

My brain is a lump of tar. My breath tastes sour. Though I gulped down a decaliter of tap water in the bathroom, my throat still burns with thirst.

I slip back into bed, taking care not to wake Sister Lucille. I stretch out, my face close to hers. The pillow is cool from the air-conditioning. The warm scent of gardenias rises from the base of her throat. A sunbeam poking through a pinprick in one of the blackout curtains inches up her body. What a miraculous world this is, where something like this can happen to someone like me.

No, not to someone *like* me. To me.

A humble soulsaver Chosen by the Shepherdess. Like my mother was Chosen by Jimmy Divine. Will you look at me?

And last night.

Last night was incredibly exciting and very different than with Angela.

I think about that.

Different. But . . . not better.

I think some more, trying to sort out my jumbled feelings. It is not easy. In so short a time, I have been bombarded with so many new ideas, each one in conflict with something I always believed was true and right and changeless, that I cannot think straight. Despite my confusion, though, there is one thing I do understand clearly.

I love Angela.

It may have taken a while to penetrate this thick skull of mine, but it is the truth.

Did we rush into marriage without knowing as much as we should have about each other? Sure we did. There is no denying it. But with the world in its final countdown, who does not leap before he looks nowadays? Still, we must have sensed some deep affinity, perceived something truly simpático between us, because we just feel right together. There is no denying that, either.

I love Angela. More than that, she is my soulmate.

Now that I stop to think about it, I see there is a lot about Angela to love, and I do not just mean her great face and those long legs. I love that she is smarter than I am, and sees things more clearly. I love that she is beautiful in body *and* soul. I love that she is a good woman who tries to live a righteous life. And I love that she loves me, and looks out for me always, although I cannot help wondering what I have done to deserve her.

I consider the Shepherdess, and ask myself what I will tell Angela about her and what happened between us. The Shepherdess said there was no sin—she said I was acting as an instrument of the Lord—and the Shepherdess does not lie, so I know Angela will understand. But I cannot help thinking she will still be hurt when she finds out.

This whole thing should be simple, but it feels awfully

complicated. Acting as God's instrument, apparently, is not free of trouble.

The sunbeam touches the Shepherdess's face. She moans in her sleep, and shields her eyes with her arm. Now I am eyeballing an armpit sporting a five o'clock shadow. I grin ruefully. Count on reality to bring you crashing back to earth. She is human after all. Three beauty marks stand out against her pale skin. They are evenly spaced and look identical. How odd. My curiosity gets the better of me, and I stick my nose practically into her underarm to get a better look.

I know now why they say curiosity killed the cat. For a moment, my heart stops.

Those are not beauty marks. They are numbers. The numerals 666. The Mark of the Beast, etched in ebony on the Shepherdess's ivory flesh.

God help me.

4∅

I goose the FreezVan. The flywheel hums. The Children and I speed away from El Morro.

As soon as we leave the abandoned grounds, we run into the thick traffic that clogs the narrow arteries of the Old City. Crawling east along the oceanfront, we barely make any headway. To our left, the Atlantic scarcely moves, either. It looks like a rippled mirror tinted a foreboding gray. To our right, ancient two-, three-, and four-story Spanish colonial houses huddle shoulder to shoulder, their pastel-and-white facades of plastered brick chipped and peeling, the intricate wrought-iron balustrades that encircle their cozy balconies rusting. At the far end of Boulevard Del Valle, the sun is topping the ramparts of El Morro's sister fort, San Cristóbal. The smog today is so thick, you can stare right at the sun without protective lenses. It looks like a Communion wafer pasted against the sky. This is going to be a muggy day.

On the seats next to me, Emma and Noel bounce up and down, excited by our spur-of-the-moment adventure. Almost immediately, though, they slip out of their safety harnesses and begin exploring the van and poking into its equipment without so much as a by-your-leave. Moments later, they are shrieking and hitting each other like any ordinary preteener brother and sister. Frankly, I am in no mood for this. It annoys me. These two little brats may be the Children of God, but they are no angels. Has no one ever taught them how to behave?

I am in a foul mood. Stumbling upon the Shepherdess's terrible secret put the fear of Lucifer in me. More, it sickened me to the core. I felt disgusted, nauseated, dirty. I wanted to bolt, scream, do *something*. But I forced myself to suit up and get out without waking her. Now, my mind is flipped topsy-turvy, I have a pounding headache, I have been wearing this same grungy jumpsuit for more than forty-eight hours, and my mouth tastes sour.

"If you two are who you claim, this is your chance to prove it," I growl. "And get back in your seats, both of you."

"Blessèd are those who believe without seeing," Noel says, meekly slipping back into his safety harness.

Smart-ass.

"But twice blessèd are those who have witnessed the truth, for their faith is solid twice over," Emma adds.

Is she mocking me? I flick her an angry glance. Her frank, steady gaze startles me. I cover by quickly looking back at the road.

Finally, we pull out of the Old City. Entering Puerta de Tierra, which gets its name from the gate that used to be on its landward side back when San Juan was a walled city, we whiz down the reserved lane, siren yodeling. I notice how Emma takes her own sweet time about clambering back into her safety harness. Traffic around us creeps. Heat waves shimmer up from ten thousand broiling vehicles—broken-down hulks, beat-up trucks, telescoping buses, tired multi-tankers, shiny new luxury vans. The rippling air makes my temples throb. I block out the resentful faces of the martyred drivers and passengers forever condemned to the penance lanes. I have my own problems.

At San Francisco, I lead the Children briskly down the corridor. Emma and Noel skip along beside me, each one clutching one of my hands. My brain is a dull blob, my belly a hive of apprehension.

The corridor boils with activity. Techs rush equipment this way and that. Médicos confer hastily as they stride from one resurrection room to the next. Orderlies sprint to answer a torrent of urgent summonses over the public address system. Six times, the Children and I have to flatten ourselves against the wall to let emergency personnel pass. A harried-looking floor nurse glances back at us with a puzzled look, but does not stop. Otherwise, nobody pays us any mind.

The freeze room. I barge in through the swinging doors, the Twins in tow. Ramírez, Cecilia, intercepts us, alarmed.

"Bless you, Brother, is something wrong?" she asks.

The room's sharp chill cuts through my clothing. "Bless

you, Sister," I say before my teeth can start to chatter. "These children want to see their mother." The orderly looks lost. "My partner. Muñoz, Fabiola."

The orderly frowns. "But these are not her children."

I am not normally a violent person, but a sickening unease has taken root in me. Maybe it is the knowledge that I slept with . . . When I picture those numerals in my mind's eye, I feel sick, violated, angry . . . I slam the orderly up against a row of lockers. Her head bounces on metal, her eyes fill with tears. My forearm crushes her breastbone, pinning her.

My voice comes out low and menacing. "Just zip it and do what I say, Sister." I am shocked at myself.

This rough stuff feels good.

Emma grabs my elbow. "Stop, Brother Juan," she says. "We forbid you to do this woman harm."

Noel interposes himself between the orderly and me. "She is one of us," he says.

I let her go. "She's a New Christer?"

She crumples to her knees, and makes the Sign of the Twins.

I step away, mechanically return the greeting.

She gets to her feet. "How can I serve the Children?"

The air in the room is icier than I remember. My entire body is trembling. I am surprised the Children are not shivering in their thin tropical robes.

"We have come for Fabiola Muñoz," Emma says. The words leave her lips as small white puffs.

The orderly taps a button. An electric whir. The drawer

holding Fabiola slides out. She is still encased in frost. Her face is still frozen in pain. I shudder at the sight. The agony she must have endured, knowing what they were doing to her and powerless to stop them.

"Poor Sister Fabiola," Emma says. "How you have suffered for your faith."

"Can you resurrect her?" I say.

That is the point of this exercise, is it not? I know now who the Shepherdess really is. I want to be just as certain who these kiddies are. This is their chance to prove themselves.

"Do you still doubt yourself?" Noel asks. He is unruffled, impervious to the cold.

I shake my head. "It's you two I have doubts about."

The boy fixes me with sympathetic eyes. "In your heart, you know who we are," he says. "But you do not yet know who *you* are, and you still fear to trust your instincts."

Just what I need to hear. Psychobabble from the mouths of babes.

Down the hall, a muffled commotion. Pounding, yelling, shrieking alarms. Cecilia Ramírez pops outside through the swinging doors and risks a quick peep.

I hear footsteps, running. Headed our way.

She lunges back inside. "A band of Angels, coming fast!" She wrestles the doors shut, bangs a metal crossbar into place.

Emma is unfazed. "Tell Fabiola it is time we left," she says.

I stare at her. "Are you talking to me?"

She nods. Noel nods.

"Are you dinged?" I say. "*I* can't resurrect her. I'm just an ordinary soulsaver. You two are supposed to be the Children of God. You two are supposed to do this."

"All men are children of God, Juan Bautista," Emma says. "All are belovèd in the eyes of the Lord." She takes my hand, looks up at me. "But you especially, Juan. That is why we have sought you out."

"You are wrestling with your faith," Noel says. "You have doubts and feel a terrible guilt for having them." He takes my other hand, holds my gaze with his. "That proves you are human and not some robot that believes because it was ordered to. Do you understand?"

I try to pull my hands free, but the Twins will not let go. "I can't bring her back," I say, agitated. "I don't have the power."

"You believe in God, don't you?" Emma asks.

I nod. Of course I do.

"Then you have the power."

I look at Fabiola. She is iced meat, a corpsicle.

"Go on," Noel says.

My lips are numb. My bones ache from the cold. "Wake up, Fabiola," I mumble. I feel like a fool.

Nothing happens.

Why would it? I am no miracle worker. I have no such power. I hear sirens outside, people running, shouting.

I shut them out, try to concentrate. But on what? My faith? My friend Fabiola? The cold fear in my belly?

I close my eyes and strain—what I'm straining I do not

know—but I seem to feel something happening, something gathering, something.

Cold burns me, bites, pierces me like thorns, stings like bees, like whips, like nettles.

Something is swelling inside me, devouring me from the inside.

I am afraid.

a c.l.e.a.n w.h.i.t.e g.l.o.w
l.i.k.e t.h.e l.i.g.h.t f.r.o.m f.l.o.w.e.r.s b.l.o.o.m.i.n.g
f.l.o.w.s t.h.r.o.u.g.h m.y b.l.o.o.d
a b.r.i.g.h.t w.h.i.t.e f.l.a.m.e
l.i.k.e t.h.e t.o.n.g.u.e.s o.f t.i.g.e.r.s s.t.a.l.k.i.n.g
l.i.c.k.s a.w.a.y m.y f.l.e.s.h
s.u.n.l.i.g.h.t s.w.i.r.l.s i.n s.p.i.r.a.l.s
a.n.d u.n.c.o.i.l.s i.n.s.i.d.e m.y e.y.e.s
a p.u.r.e c.l.e.a.n v.o.i.c.e
s.i.n.g.s l.o.v.e
s.i.n.g.s j.o.y
s.i.n.g.s l.o.v.e
s.i.n.g.s j.o.y
s.i.n.g.s

Fabiola's eyes open.

Clean, bright, blue, aglow.

They shine. They recognize.

My lungs labor. My belly aches. My head is light and airy, vast enough to contain planets.

Fabiola, incandescent, sits up and smiles.

Reverberating across a vast distance, a voice inside me cries, "How can this be, this be, this be?"

The tides of light and confusion subside.

"You came for me," Fabiola says. Simply, with gratitude.

I have witnessed a miracle. More, I may have, God help me, performed it. I am stunned.

In the corridor outside, bedlam, sirens, voices, banging against our door. It bends, quivers, but the bar holds. For now.

Fabiola, Cecilia, and I exchange looks. The Twins seem unconcerned. My head pounds, but I ignore it.

"There is a back way to the basement," Cecilia whispers.

She rushes us out through a maintenance hatch and down an unpainted metal stairwell. Our boot heels clang and echo.

Two levels below, we sprint into a large basement, a labyrinth of pipes, heating and cooling ducts, catwalks, and grids. Cecilia guides us through the maze, weaving her way toward an exit at the far end.

"That leads outside," she says. "It will be a few minutes before anyone remembers this rear access. Go on now, hurry."

"Aren't you coming?" I say.

"I can't. I have a daughter at home."

"But what about the Angels? They won't look kindly on your helping us escape."

"I'll say you muscled me. They understand intimidation."

I flash the Sign of the Twins. "Bless you, Sister," I say. It hardly seems enough.

We run.

41

Long time ago in Bethlehem,
So the Holy Bible say,
Mary's boy child, Jesus Christ,
Was born on Christmas Day.

This Christmas Eve is even warmer than usual for a tropical night in December. Cristóbal sits on the ground by the gates to El Morro, curled around his cuatro, sweat beading his forehead. His half-starved comrades prepare their meager rations over scattered cook fires in the courtyard. Not for them any of the seasonal delicacies the archbishop will be enjoying in his private dining room. No traditional roast pig on a spit with crisp cracklings and all the trimmings. No deep-fried stuffed pig entrails, the dark, spicy morcilla that melts in the mouth and tingles on the tongue. No delicately flavored boiled bananas bathed in virgin olive oil. No tasty arroz con gandules that Mainlanders call rice with black-eyed peas. And no sweet tembleque pudding freckled with mouthwatering cinnamon for dessert. For these poor folk, only codfish fritters and bread. If they are lucky.

Wood smoke tickles my nose. Outside the fortress walls, the muffled crash of waves serves as a reminder that San Ignacio, a powerful out-of-season hurricane that narrowly missed the Island, is still sidling by only a hundred miles to the north. A fuzzy moon rides low in the sky, and salt spray mists the air.

The five double strings of Cristóbal's cuatro ring out in the still night. Pentecost sprawls on the flagstones, head pillowed on his master's thigh. A massive yawn exposes the monster's yellow teeth. From the door of the Children's room, I listen to Cristóbal sing, marveling at how such an ugly man can be blessed with so lovely a voice, and how everyone seems to have at least one wonderful or terrible quality about him that no one else would suspect.

> *Trumpets sound and angels sing,*
> *A new king born today,*
> *And man will live forevermore*
> *Because of Christmas Day.*

I keep thinking about what happened in Cecilia Ramírez's freeze room at San Francisco, wondering what it means, asking myself how I managed to work a miracle. Now that the rush of emotions has receded, I can't help questioning if it really was me. I mean, when you come right down to it, all I did was say: "Wake up, Fabiola." And with how much conviction? Sure, I wanted it to work, maybe more than anything at that moment, but how can three words from a nobody bring back a bifreeze when the world's most advanced technology cannot?

I believe in miracles. My father heals the blind, the lame, and the halt all the time. So do a host of others like him. Preacher Pat. La Hermana Emanuela. Father Flash. Little Jesus Junior. It is a major section of their résumés. But folks who work miracles like the original Jesus are a different breed from thee and me. To become fit channels for God's power, they must first achieve great holiness. Jimmy Divine ranks as top dog among that pack of healers, but even he has never raised anyone from the dead.

Let us make no bones about it: this humble servant ranks pretty low among the holy. So how could I suddenly have beaten my father at his own game? Could the whole thing have been rigged, a Passion playlet staged for my benefit to get me to switch over to the Children's side? I do not think the possibility is so far-fetched. Look at the other people involved: Fabiola, Cecilia Ramírez, Father René— confessed New Christers all. Makes you wonder.

But why try to dupe *me*? What is there to be gained? Do they suspect I am working for the archbishop? What would they do to me if they knew? Jimmy Divine's only begotten son. What might that be worth to them?

My head aches. I am not cut out for this, trying to figure out what is going on beneath the surface of things.

Angela could manage it. She would cut to the bone in a flash. Yes, I should talk this over with Angela.

I slip back inside.

Flickering torch flames make the walls seem to shiver and sway. Where time has chipped away at their ancient mortar, rough bricks made of red clay peep out. In the corner, María de Dios, the Twins' mother, tends a homemade hibachi, frying cod fritters and a handful of ripe bananas in a small pan of smoking hot peanut oil.

Emma sits on the floor, playing trompo. The rules of the game are simple. Spin a wooden top and roll a dozen dice. Cull out the ones, then scoop up the rest and roll again, trying to collect all twelve before the top falters. Then, do the same with the twos, threes, fours, fives, and sixes.

Emma sets the top spinning. "You must do it, Juan Bautista," she says. She rolls the dice.

I cannot believe what I am hearing. We had settled this.

"How can I betray you to the Shepherdess after you've shown me who you are?" I say.

"Because it is your part in the Plan."

María de Dios dispenses crispy breaded codfish, along with chunks of hot, crusty bread. Emma waves her share away. Noel nibbles gingerly at the sizzling fritters, trying to keep from burning his lips or tongue. Fabiola tears into her food like she has not eaten in days. Which, come to think of it, she hasn't. I toy with mine.

It is weird how this is working out. The Children want me to do exactly what my father and the archbishop want.

"But if I do as you say, I'll be like Judas."

Emma nods without breaking the rhythm of her game. "In a way." Her fingers dart among the dice while the top

204

spins. "He had his part to play so that one of the prophecies would be fulfilled, and now you have yours."

"Judas weakened afterward, though," Noel says. "He let doubt conquer him before the Resurrection, and took his own life. But he repented and was forgiven, and sits at the right hand of the Father alongside his Brother Apostles."

"Is that a fact?" I'd always wondered about that.

"What lies ahead for you is not easy, Juan Bautista," Emma says. She culls out the threes, sweeps the rest into the leather cup. "But we ask no more of you than we know you can give." The dice clatter back onto the floor.

Fabiola wolfs down the last of her ration, and gestures inquiringly at mine. I give her my untouched fritter and bread crust. She digs in.

"This is some sort of test, isn't it?" I ask.

Noel sucks on his greasy fingers.

"Perhaps you need to test yourself," Emma says.

She is this close to finishing foursies when the trompo clatters to a stop. That used to drive me nuts when I was a kiddy. Emma calmly spins the top and goes back to onesies.

I return to the door. People have gathered around the gatekeeper. Pentecost dozes.

> *Hark now, hear the angels sing:*
> *"A new king born today,*
> *And man will live forevermore*
> *Because of Christmas Day."*

I lift my eyes to the soft winter sky, imagine the Star of Bethlehem on that long-ago night when the Son of God was born. What a time that must have been, a sun blazing in the night sky, miracles loose in the world.

Three stars catch my eye. Astronomers call them the Belt of Orion. Islanders know them as los Reyes Magos, the Magi, because they appear at Christmastime to proclaim the Coming of the Lord.

I do not want to do what the Children ask. Especially if they are who they claim and seem to be. Betrayal is such a contemptible sin. Even if Judas Iscariot was forgiven in Heaven, on earth men despise him still. And if Emma and Noel *are* the Antichrists, I surely want to do nothing that will help them.

I am trapped between two powerful forces, and do not know which camp I belong in.

I could take the archbishop's advice and follow the example of Jesus: Thy will be done. But I am sick of being pummeled by events, with no control over where I am headed.

And then there is this. It is becoming increasingly clear to me that the world is nothing like what I was taught to believe. Look at how much I have already found out that I never knew or even suspected. How much more is there that I still do not know?

And what about my "miracle"?

It was like a tumult of light inside me. And afterward, a sweet light-headedness, like fingers stroking my brain. I would like to feel that way again.

Seagulls strut atop the gates to El Morro, their white feathers blue in the moonlight. The ocean falls momentarily silent, a lull in which to eavesdrop on secrets the sea breeze whispers. The scent of salt spray floats in the air. Across the courtyard, Pentecost lifts his massive head and yawns. By the flicker of firelight, Cristóbal surveys the crowd of neighbors and friends who surround him.

"Merry Christmas, Brothers and Sisters," Cristóbal says, then plucks the strings of his cuatro and sings.

> *And man will live forevermore*
> *Because of Christmas Day.*

Why do I remember eyes the color of wet tea leaves?

42

"So who do I side with? The Children or the Shepherdess?"

I have told Angela about the miracle I performed, the betrayal the Twins want me to carry out on their behalf, the doubts assailing me—which now seem to encompass everything and everybody—and my indecision. I conclude with how I have come for her to dispel my confusion.

I sit on our bed, waiting for the illumination I know her answer will bring. Angela stares at the floor. I feel better just knowing that her mind is wrestling with my problems.

A mess of rattlesnakes writhing inside a wicker basket fills the wall screen. The sound is muted. The freckled face of Preacher Pat Spangler, Mr. God's Number One Snake Handler, comes on. Sweat beads his bald head. Preacher Pat puts on a good show, and tonight's live transmission from the newly dedicated Shrine of Saint Elvis in Memphis is

going to be something special. Graceland. Was that a pro-
phetic name or what?

Angela looks up. "I don't know what to tell you." Her
eyes are full of sympathy and apology.

I cannot believe this. Angela sees everything. She sizes
up a situation before I am even aware it exists. How can she
not know?

"Well, whose side are *you* on?" I ask.

"No one's. I don't know. Yours."

In Memphis, Mr. God's Number One Snake Handler
dances across the stage carrying a sassy viper at arm's
length. The snake's tail twitches. Its tongue flicks. Preacher
Pat hollers and screams at it—in tongues, I imagine; it is
hard to tell with the sound squelched. The snake's unblink-
ing eyes never leave his florid face.

"How can you be on my side when I don't know which
side I'm on?" I ask.

I am shaken. I would have bet my life that Angela would
side with the Shepherdess. It makes you wonder if you
really know the folks you think you know. Still, I used to
see myself as a bedrock of faith, and look at me now. And
as for Angela, didn't she shock me the night she wanted us
to shuck our marriage robes?

Preacher Pat releases the snake's head. The diamond-
back coils itself around his bare arm, slithers over his shoulder, wraps itself around his neck. I would be dumping in my
jumpsuit, but Preacher Pat just eyes the beast with the contempt the Devil's brethren deserve. Why the rattler does

not fang him while it has the chance is one of the mysteries that make Christianity wondrous.

"For some reason, Juan Bautista," Angela says, "you've decided you're not smart enough to tell right from wrong. But that's not so." She moves closer, takes my hand, strokes it while she speaks. "You're a good man, Juan. That's why I believe in you." She puts my hand on her belly, which is firm and round as a volleyball. "That's why I believe you'll be a good father to this child for whatever time we may have left together on earth and for eternity thereafter." Then she places my palm against the smoothness of her face. "And that's why I believe that whatever you decide, you'll be on the right side." She releases me, clasps her hands together over her beautiful belly. "But this is one road you have to walk by yourself."

The rattler chomps Preacher Pat's chubby cheek.

I cannot believe it. Preacher Pat has never been bitten. His eyes pop. His lips form a small O of disbelief. He and the snake plunge out of the picture.

A graphic crawls across the empty wall screen: *"Preacher Pat: Live from Memphis is experiencing technical difficulties. Please pray with us."*

When the picture returns, the stage is crawling with panicked rattlers. Somebody must have knocked over their basket. The whirring from a hundred or more snakes must be awesome, but people in choir robes are wading in and hacking at the creatures with fire axes. Could this be part of the show?

"Aha," I say.

Angela looks at me strangely. "What is it?"

"I just realized there's a way I can straddle the fence a little longer," I tell her.

"What?" Angela asks. Then the clarity of understanding fills her eyes. "By doing what both sides want you to do anyway," she whispers.

Didn't I say she was smart?

43

"—in a humble manger," the Shepherdess says from the giant public viddy screen, addressing the ragged street people gathered in the park, "and today we celebrate the day when God sent His only begotten Son to die for our sins."

Even though it is Christmas morning, I have a meeting with the archbishop at nine-thirty. I have arrived too early, so I am killing a half hour in El Parque de las Palomas. The cozy pocket park gets its name from the flocks of doves that nest in its leafy banyan trees and in the Swiss cheese of pigeonholes cut into the ancient wall of El Castillo de Santa Catalina, which houses the offices of the archbishop. The doves are protected by strict law. Otherwise, the starving would kill and eat them.

I recall the Christmas Eves of my childhood. No visions of sugarplums danced in *my* head. When I was a young boy, my crèche mates and I would ride excitedly to La Catedral in the Old City to hear Misa de Gallo, Midnight Mass, sung in majestic Latin. I remember how the music would merge into a mighty voice whose beauty gladdened my heart. I imagined this grand heartsong swelling to fill the narthex, the nave, the transept, and the chancel, then soaring up through the rotunda and ascending to kiss the Ear of God Himself.

Golden flames danced atop fat altar candles. Acolytes and attendants in snowy robes would line up in neat rows to either side of the main altar with heads bowed, while seasoned priests and priestesses in white Christmas array celebrated the birth of God's Child—the most glorious moment in the history of humankind.

And I would feel grateful and at one with our Father.

When we reached home again following services, our stomachs would rumble from having fasted to receive Communion. In the crèche cafeteria, the nuns would bring us steaming mugs of cocoa with crusty chunks of fresh-baked pan criollo and thick slices of golden queso de papa. And when we finally went to bed at two or three in the morning, we would find a gift from el Niñito Jesús tucked under a corner of our pillows. A tin of hard candy, each piece shaped to resemble a saint or martyr; maybe a handful of figs in a bag of fine mesh; a rustic Christmas angel sculpted in reddish clay; or a shiny ceramic shepherd holding a carved wooden crook. We would drift off to dreamland with a smile on our lips and the Christ Child's gift clutched in our fist. And we would awaken on Christmas Day without a care in our heads.

If only life could be that simple now.

"This year Christmas is more special than ever," the Shepherdess says, "because this, my children, will be the last Christmas."

That is meant as an uplifting thought, but it chills me instead.

"Six days from now," the Shepherdess says, eyes shining beatifically, "as we ring out the last and final century of man's earthly sojourn, we will witness the Second Coming, and the righteous shall be seized by the Rapture."

I have been in my jumpsuit for three days straight. My skin itches. My hair is greasy and stringy. My mouth tastes like crap.

"Think of it," the Shepherdess whispers.

I think of the unrighteous, who are to be left behind on a world literally become a Hell on earth.

My flesh crawls.

44

The bowl of rotting apples has disappeared from the archbishop's desk, but a faint scent of decay lingers. I tell him where to find the Children.

"Bless you, Juan Bautista!" he says, beaming. "That is the best Christmas gift this old priest ever had." With that warm smile and those chubby cheeks, he looks like a cherub, although, because of the overnight growth of beard, a slightly sleazy one. I wonder what could have been so pressing this morning that it kept him from shaving. He scoops up a red satphone from the intricately carved Spanish credenza behind him and whispers a code name, then, while he waits for a response, says to me, "I will see that a band of Angels scrambles for the old fort immediately."

I take no joy in the announcement, but Malpica does not notice. He speaks urgently into the phone.

He hangs up and beams at me again. "Your father will be pleased when he hears of your success, Brother Juan." He leans back expansively in a high-backed black leather chair. "Everything is going according to plan."

I look up. "What plan is that?" I ask.

A smile plays over the archbishop's lips. "Why Divine Plan, of course."

Is he serious, or was that meant as a joke? Whichever, he looks very . . . what? Relieved? Self-satisfied? Amused?

Or is he mocking me?

Malpica waddles around the desk and claps me heartily on the back.

"You, son, should be happy and proud."

Maybe he is right. But someone once said sin is what you feel bad after, and at this moment I feel far from good.

45

The December sun is sultry, and I am dripping with sweat as I battle through the crowds clogging Calle del Cristo. I force my way up the hill past La Catedral and the old Convento Dominicano, which, we were told in Sunday school, was remodeled into a tourist hotel called El Convento a little past the midpoint of the last century.

Can you imagine? The high-ceilinged chapel where modestly garbed Dominican nuns used to perform their daily devotions was converted into a bar and supper club where wild-maned Gypsies from Andalucía in body-hugging dresses of red, violet, and green sang the Moorish canto jondo and stamped their heels in the intricate, sensual zapateado of the flamenco as they whirled and swayed to the rasgueado of guitars and the clack of castanets.

Just off the inner courtyard, the former refectory of the convent was made into an opulent gaming casino, where the Godless people of that time pitted their luck against one-armed gambling robots and tried to predict whether a spinning white ball would fall into a black or red slot. It puts me in mind of the time Our Savior was forced to cast the money changers out of the temple. I guess such lessons are lost on subsequent generations.

Making progress up the narrow sidewalks of Calle del Cristo is almost impossible. The cobblestoned street itself is impassable. It is clogged with vehicles lined up bumper to bumper from the statue of Ponce de León—the Island's first governor—that graces Plaza San José at the top of the hill all the way to the corner of Fortaleza Street, where everyone must make a left turn a block short of the tiny Capilla del Cristo at the bottom of the hill. I elbow people aside, too intent on my mission to worry about manners. A few turn on me angrily, but hold their tongue when they see my uniform.

I know the notion is crazy after what I have just done, but I have this idea that if I warn the Children in time, that will somehow prevent any harm from coming to them.

Behind the statue of Ponce de León at the top of Calle del Cristo stands the simple white Iglesia San José, the oldest church in the western hemisphere. As I bull my way through the crowd outside the church, a husky street preacher grabs my shoulders and demands to know if I have been washed in the Blood of the Lamb. I break free and angle toward the abandoned access road to El Morro. The street preacher shrieks at me not to enter. His followers give chase, but I have a head start and lose them in the tall brush that borders the buckled asphalt.

No one will come after me. A month ago, I would not have gone in here myself.

I struggle through the underbrush, matting my uniform with cockleburs. Sweat streams down my chest, back, and sides, soaking my jumpsuit and my underwear. A sea breeze rustles the palm trees and brushes my skin, providing mild relief from the heat as I stride along the bumpy, broken remains of the old fort's access road. Minutes later, I clatter across the stone arch bridging the moat and hammer on the gates of the fort. I bend over to catch my breath. The salt spray misting the air clogs my laboring lungs.

In the sky, bedlam breaks loose. Powerful engines roar. A great wind blasts. The ground shakes.

My heart races. The gates open a crack, and Cristóbal's good eye peers out. Hastily, I sidle through and rush down the connecting alleyway toward the courtyard. Hands clamped over their ears, people emerge from their shelters. From the far side of the courtyard, Fabiola throws me a wave.

Thrusters howling, a helojet troop carrier as shiny and black as polished onyx sweeps in from the seaward side of the fort. Avenging Angels in black ride in its personnel pods, armed with rods of Aaron—those short brass military staffs that can stun a person on contact or fire a disabling energy ball.

María de Dios runs out of one of the blockhouses. Even from this distance, I can see the fear on her face.

Like a monstrous dragonfly, the troop carrier dances in through updrafts, its jets screaming. Wind shear threatens to smash it into the outer wall, but it stabilizes, rights itself and roars on in.

Cristóbal sprints across the courtyard, robes snapping, face inflamed with rage, mouth agape in a drowned-out shout.

A second helojet booms up from below the parapets, swoops down on the tail of the first one.

Where are the Children?

Cristo, there they are, out in the open, exposed. Hair streaming, they watch the incoming troop carriers muscle their way down into the courtyard.

María de Dios struggles toward the Children, her robe cracking like a bullwhip in the hellish wind.

At the heart of a storm of dirt and garbage, the helojets roll and buck in place scarcely three meters above the courtyard. The racket is deafening.

María de Dios throws her arms around the Children, pulls them close.

The Angels vault from their pods. They hit the ground running and fan out, a well-oiled military machine just starting to warm up.

Tears roll down María de Dios's cheeks. Emma and Noel nestle against her. Fabiola and Cristóbal try to reach them, fighting the rotor blasts.

Like Lot's wife, I stand stolid, immobile. I cannot bring myself to move, only watch.

One detachment of Angels surrounds the Children and

the three adults, while a second roughly herds the other onlookers up against the walls.

The helojets yo-yo up into the sky. The merciless
Christmas sun glints and sparks off their smoked plasteel
control bubbles and black enameled insect bodies. The
throb of their engines fades into the background. The pandemonium engulfing us springs from human throats now.

An Angel levels his rod at the Children.

The voices choke off. The sky throbs with the pulse
of the helos. María de Dios whimpers. Then suddenly
Cristóbal whips out a machete from the folds of his robes,
and before even the most trigger-happy of the Shepherdess's Heavenly Guardians can react, he hacks off the
Angel's hand at the wrist.

Emma shouts, "No!" But the deed is done.

The Angel's weapon crashes to the flagstones. Screaming, he mashes the spurting stump into his armpit, frantically squeezes to stop the bleeding. But the blood gushes,
spurts like wine over his sleeve and leg and turns his silver
insignia scarlet.

Shoving and kicking and taking the Name of Our Lord
in vain, his squadmates pummel the onlookers to the
ground, clubbing anyone who tries to rise.

The injured Angel screams and sobs. Then his howls
stop. His eyes roll up, and he crumples to the ground.

Enraged Angels pile on Cristóbal. They kick the machete from his hand, bash him with their rods. Pentecost
springs to the defense of his master, but a stunbolt cuts him
down.

I watch in horror.

Emma rushes to the side of the unconscious Angel. His face is ashen, drenched in sweat. He moans. Noel examines the man's stump. Blood still pumps from it.

Tears well in the boy's eyes. He exchanges a look with his sister. Tears begin to roll down Emma's cheeks.

The Angels continue to kick and punch Cristóbal. No mercy. The gatekeeper sprawls unconscious, his face a mask of blood. His good eye is swollen shut.

"Burn the sinner!" orders the Archangel.

An Angel shoves the business end of his weapon into the gatekeeper's battered face.

Noel says, "No."

He does not shout or raise his voice, yet the word brings the Angels to a halt. Everyone turns to see who has spoken with such authority.

"He has harmed no one," Noel says.

"He has maimed one of my best men!" rasps the Archangel, a muscular, angry specimen with a lean, wolfish face and the look of a man with an appetite for trouble. "Get away from him!"

Emma pays him no heed. "Awaken, belovèd of God," she commands the maimed Angel.

The man's eyes open. He is dazed. With Emma and Noel's help, he sits up. Bewildered, he buries his face in his hands.

And pulls his hands away.

The hand is reattached to his wrist.

He goggles at it, makes a fist, spreads his fingers. Mouth open, he examines his hand front and back.

"¡Milagro!" he exclaims, half in joy, half in fear.

Cristóbal's comrades look exalted, vindicated. The Angel's squadmates stare in awe.

"Do what you came for," Emma says to the Archangel.

"I give the orders here, child!" the Archangel barks, but without his earlier arrogance. To his men he says, "Release him."

They drop Cristóbal, who slumps senseless to the ground. Emma and Noel hurry to minister to him.

The Archangel stabs a furious finger at the Twins. "Load them on the helos!"

His men hesitate.

"Do not be fooled by their Devil tricks," the Archangel rasps. "Lucifer has no power over the anointed."

Still the Angels hang back.

The Archangel flushes. He toggles his rod of Aaron, triggering on ominous hum. He levels the staff at his men. Fear spreads over their faces, and they begin to move toward the Twins, but gingerly.

The Children ignore this. Their tiny fingers stroke the gatekeeper's head and body. His groaning subsides, but he is still a bloody mess.

"Take them!" the Archangel shouts. "Now!"

He fires an energy bolt over the heads of his men. A panicky surge forward. When finally the Angels lay nervous hands on them, the Children allow themselves to be taken without resistance.

I am filled with dread.

46

"What did you do with her body?" Jimmy Divine says.

I have been summoned back to the archbishop's office. My father sits behind the archbishop's desk in the high-backed leather chair. The archbishop stands to one side.

Malpica looks taller than I remember. And...wobbly. Then I glimpse his tiny black shoes peeking out from beneath his black hassock: he is teetering on the three-inch soles and heels of a pair of clerical lifts. Why is the archbishop suddenly striving for height? Is it simple vanity or the larger-than-life presence of Jimmy Divine?

"Wake up, boy!" Jimmy Divine shouts, snapping me out of my reverie. "Where is her body?"

"Whose body?" I ask. Cristo, are they on to me?

"Your partner's," Jimmy Divine says impatiently. "The one with the persecution complex."

It strikes me that the closer I stick to the truth, the easier it should be to dissemble. When I speak, I try to keep my gaze steady and my voice even. Turns out, it is not as hard as I had expected.

"I . . . took it to the Children and challenged them to prove themselves by resurrecting her," I say.

Jimmy Divine leans forward, gives me a hard look. Has he seen through me? "And did they?" he asks.

"No . . ."

Jimmy Divine leans back in the chair and clasps his hands together behind his head. His smile is so warm and sincere, you cannot help loving the guy.

"So then you knew." Seeing my puzzlement, he adds, "That they were Children of the Father of Lies."

"Oh," I say. How to phrase this? "Well, yes, sir, then I knew the truth."

Jimmy Divine nods. "For a while there, you were kind of slipslidin' on over to the other side, weren't you now, boy?" He gives me that charm-you-out-of-your-socks grin, full force.

Uh-oh. This could be treacherous ground. I decide the honest-but-contrite route is the least risky path. "I guess maybe I was, a little, yes, sir."

"Sure you were." Jimmy Divine puffs an aromatic Cohiba to life, and stabs the cigar at Malpica. The archbishop does not seem to appreciate the heady smell. Jimmy Divine shakes his cheroot chidingly. "All that guilty-conscience garbage you were downloadin' on poor Brother Tony."

The archbishop waves the matter off, taking advantage of the gesture to fan away what he can of the cigar smoke.

It also looks to me like he is not used to standing, especially on those extra-thick elevator platforms, and is getting fed up with it.

"I was Connie Confused," I say.

"That's the trouble," Jimmy Divine says. "Lots of 'Connie Confused' folks have let themselves be conned by these slicktalkin' kiddies." The Cohiba is really stinking up the office. "Only now we are gonna expose them."

"How are you going to do that?" I ask, trying not to breathe through my nose.

"Did you know my Special Edition New Year's Eve show's goin' out global?"

I shake my head.

"That's right," Jimmy Divine says. "The whole world will be watchin'." He leans forward, jabs his cigar at me for emphasis. "That is where we'll expose those kiddies for what they are." He flops back in the chair, rocks back and forth with a self-satisfied look, rolling thick smoke around in his mouth, savoring the moment along with his Cohiba. "Gonna be good, son," he says with a wink. "Trust me. Gonna be *real* good."

"I'll be watching," I say, fighting the tickle in my nose.

"Whole blessèd *world* will be watchin'. Ain't that so, Brother Tony?"

Malpica grins. "Amen, Brother Jimmy. A-blessèd-men to that."

I sneeze.

47

"*You* have a date with destiny tonight on *It's Jimmy Divine Time! The Special Edition!*" Brother Conn Darden cries over my headband. "Join us live and in person for the Second Coming and the End of the World! If it's the last thing you do, be there!"

Aguinaldos, the program of traditional Puerto Rican Christmas music that I have been listening to, has gone from playing the Amaury Veray classic "Villancico Yaucano" to running promos for viddy shows.

"Up next, America's favorite radio game show, *Beat the Prophets.*"

A knock at the door. Who could that be? Angela and I are not expecting anyone. I snuff the sound on my headband. "Come in."

The door slides open.

Cristo! A hooded figure in a black robe. My heart trip-hammers. An Avenging Angel?

Before I can react, the hooded figure steps inside. I scramble to my feet, my heart in my throat.

The figure drops the kaffiyeh that masks its face.

"Fabiola!"

But Fabiola is supposed to be hiding out at El Morro. Jimmy Divine thinks she is dead.

"What are you doing here?" I ask, the words tumbling out. "Are you dinged?"

Angela peers out from the bedroom. Her belly is huge. She takes the situation in at a glance. "This is your partner, isn't it?" she says. It is not a question. "The one you resurrected?"

I introduce them.

"I feel like I know you," Angela says. Her excitement takes me aback.

"I feel like I know you, too," Fabiola says. She speaks absently, like she has more important things on her mind. She sits. "What do you know about the Twins?" she asks me. No preamble, no small talk. "Have they been harmed?"

"Were you really dead?" Angela says. Her voice drops to a whisper. "And now you're alive again, not through science but by a miracle, like Lazarus!"

"The Children haven't been harmed," I answer Fabiola. "They want them healthy. On my father's show tonight, they plan to prove that the Children are the Antichrists."

Holding her belly, Angela lowers herself next to Fabiola. Fabiola slides over to give her more space.

"A living miracle," Angela breathes.

"How do they expect to do that?" Fabiola says to me. My stomach muscles clench. "Trial by fire."

"What are they going to do," Angela asks, aghast, "burn them at the stake?!"

"Something along those lines," I say.

"That's crazy," Fabiola says. "Why?"

"If the Children are unharmed by the flames," I say, quoting my father, "it will prove they are the Antichrists, because 'only the serpent Satan dwells in the devouring fire.'"

"And if they burn to death?" Fabiola asks.

"Then they were just a couple of misguided kiddies who tragically brought the whole thing down upon themselves."

"We've got to save them," Angela says.

I am amazed. I spend weeks wallowing in self-pity, days agonizing over doubts, while Angela overcomes a lifetime of indoctrination with one simple, clear-cut decision.

"We can't do that," I say.

Fabiola nods agreement with Angela. "We have to try, Juan Bautista," she tells me fiercely.

For a moment, I am at a loss for words. I do not really know either of these two women.

"Where is that famous faith of yours?" I finally manage. "I mean, are these the Christ Children or not?"

That seems to give Fabiola pause. She eventually nods, even if it is reluctantly.

I go on. "Would Jesus have wanted to be rescued before the Crucifixion? Would He, for example, have wanted Simon the Cyrene to create a diversion on the road to

Calvary so that He could have blended into the crowd and escaped?"

Fabiola shakes her head.

"Well, then?" I say.

Fabiola looks stubborn.

"Well, then?"

She nods.

"What will happen to them?" Angela asks.

"Whatever God wills," I answer. My words sound hollow, even to me. I change the subject. "How is Cristóbal?"

For the past six days, I have asked myself why I did not stand up for the Children like Cristóbal did, and why I did nothing while he was being beaten.

"He could be better," Fabiola says. "The Children healed his flesh but had no time to minister to his spirit. Still, Cristóbal is a strong soul. With God's help he will recover."

"You're sure sounding a lot less Sally Cynical," I say.

She tilts her head to one side and fixes me with the oddest look.

"Dying," she says, "can give a person a whole new perspective."

48

The Estadio José Nicolás Palmer is jammed with more than one hundred thousand souls, far beyond its official capacity. People fill the aisles and spill across the grassy games area. A giant stage, with orbiting lights and levicams, dominates the playing field. The thrum of a circling camera blimp's engines provides a deep-throated counterpoint to the cheery salsa rhythm of the Gospel Maniacs' latest hit.

> *Oh, there's a meetin' here tonight,*
> *There's a meetin' here tonight,*
> *I can tell by your friendly face*
> *There's a meetin' here tonight!*

Lasers etch the words IT'S JIMMY DIVINE TIME! against the night sky in glowing blue and green. It is 10:02 P.M., December 31, 2099. The last New Year's Eve of the century, perhaps the last New Year's Eve ever. One hour and fifty-eight minutes remain before the End of the World. The global feed of Jimmy Divine's *Special Edition* show is just under way. Thanks to my "connections," Angela, Fabiola, and I have three of the best seats in the house.

Onstage, the Paths of Righteousness Dancers kick up a storm. Truck-size viddy monitors flash larger-than-life images of the performers. The crowd claps along with the infectious rhythm. Bodies bump and sway. Grins grow on a hundred thousand faces.

"And now, Brothers and Sisters . . . heeeee-e-e-e-re's *Jimmy!*"

Jimmy Divine bounds onstage to thunderous applause. His image echoes and reechoes across the myriad viddy walls encircling the stage. He fields an old-fashioned wireless mike tossed by a stagehand and swings into the song.

> *Well, Satan is mad and I am glad,*
> *Lost the soul he thought he had,*
> *Satan is a liar and a conjure, too,*
> *Better watch out, brother, he'll conjure you,*
> *Conjure you, conjure you-hoo-hoo!*

"Live from San Juan, Puerto Rico!" Brother Conn intones. "*It's Jimmy Divine Time! The Special Edition!* Starring: Brother Jimmy Divine!"

Brother Jimmy drops into a split, pops back up on his toes. Who would have thought a man of his age could still boast such strength and suppleness?

"The Make a Joyful Noise unto the Lord Gospel Maniacs!"

232

The Maniacs run in countercircles, weaving in and out among themselves like ecstatic maypole dancers.

"The I Shall Walk Forever in the Path of Righteousness Dancers!"

The Dancers fly in from every corner of the stage, praising the Lord with their joyful motion.

"With special guest star, Sister Alma Lucille Ferris!"

A soft-focus medium close-up of the Shepherdess lights up the forest of screens. As the camera glides in tight, she looks into the oncoming lens with heavy-lidded eyes that promise more than Salvation.

"And later tonight," Brother Conn proclaims, building masterfully to a big finish, "you won't want to miss the Second Coming—live and in person! With extra special guest: Our Lord Jesus Christ!"

The familiar face of the Digitized Jesus flashes from viddy wall to viddy wall. Digitized stars orbit his digitized head.

The show's belovèd brass-and-banjo theme kicks off, launching the Paths of Righteousness Dancers into a mighty tap extravaganza.

> *Give me that old time religion,*
> *Give me that old time religion,*
> *Give me that old time religion,*
> *It's good enough for me!*

Twenty-four bodies move as one. Tap-tap-tap, they brush, spank, and scuff; dig, paddle, and roll. Tap-tappity-tap, they flap and stomp and shuffle and chug. In perfect synchronicity, one eye-catching combination after another, they riff and drop, ball-change and clap. We watch open-mouthed with admiration at their flawless mass precision. What fun! What joy! What a glorious example of the things folks can accomplish if they just put aside their differences and pull together!

With a fusillade of taps, the number climaxes. We fill the ensuing silence with deafening applause.

Light as air, the Dancers melt into the wings. Jimmy Divine stalks out onstage. A palpable sense of purpose adds strength to the set of his body. A touch of wild abandon glitters in his eyes.

"Brothers and Sisters," he cries out, preaching hot and heavy from word one, "we are all waitin' for the Messiah!" His voice crackles, his eyes burn. "But before the Messiah can return to us, there is somethin' *we* must do first!"

He looks around expectantly, like he is waiting for someone to tell him what that is. All eyes remain fixed on him. No one takes a stab, no one ventures a guess. In rapt, utter silence, we wait.

Jimmy Divine takes a deep breath. "Prepare ye the Way of the Lord. That's what the Good Book says." He points a commanding finger at the crowd. "Prepare ye," he repeats, breaking it down into bite-size chunks. "The Way." He stabs the finger into the air. "Of the Lord."

He nods to himself, like he is saying, Now, that's clear enough, isn't it? Then, a quizzical look comes over his face.

"But how can we do that, Brothers and Sisters?" He tilts

his head to one side. "What can you and I do to help prepare the Way?"

At least one brother among the faithful cannot restrain
himself further. "Tell us, Brother Jimmy!" he shouts, and the
crowd erupts: "Tell us, Brother Jimmy!" So much for the
virtue of patience.

Jimmy Divine grins. They are his.

"We can start, my friends, by riddin' the world of false
prophets!"

To punctuate the sentence, he claps and shouts "Hunh!"
and the crowd shouts "Hunh!" with him.

"We can start by lookin' the Antichrists in the eye, and
sendin' 'em back to Hell, where they come from!"

He claps and shouts "Hunh!" and again the crowd shouts
with him.

"Amen!" adds the lone brother. His tiny voice barely
creases the vast night air, but instantly it is multiplied ten
times tenfold as a hundred thousand voices echo fervently,
"AMEN!"

"Let me hear you say: Satan, go to Hell!" Jimmy Divine
shouts.

A hundred thousand throats chorus, "Satan, go to Hell!"
Jimmy Divine windmills his arms for more, and the crowd
takes up a chant.

"SATAN, GO TO HELL!

"SATAN, GO TO HELL!

"SATAN, GO TO HELL!"

He lowers his arms for quiet, and the last word of the

235

chant echoes and reechoes within walls that are higher and broader and thicker and stronger than any ever built to safeguard doomed Jericho—Hell, Hell, Hell—until it fades to nothing.

"But, Brothers and Sisters," Jimmy Divine shouts into the sudden silence, "just tellin' Satan don't mean nothin'! We got to ship that evil demon back to his home in Hades, one way, José, no deposit, no return, so he can't never come back! Brothers and Sisters! Do-you-want-to-do-that?"

"Yes!"

"Say it again!"

"Yes!

"Yes!

"Yes!"

"If you want to do that, give an Amen!"

"AMEN!

"AMEN!

"AMEN!"

A deep, dark musical chord shivers the night, rumbles through the living flesh of our bodies. My heart pounds, my breathing stops.

An honor guard appears, Avenging Angels marching in formation, bathed in merciless white light. Their boots glint and glisten. Their black-on-black uniforms look like living charcoal. Their faces, washed out by the light, appear as smooth and featureless as rosary beads. It takes a moment to grasp that they are escorting two white air litters bearing two tiny frost-rimed bodies.

Emma and Noel.

The dread-inspiring chord modulates and swells. Rumbles, rattles, and roars, sprung from synthetic digital throats and amplified to an earsplitting din, join in and overpower the chanted amens. I feel a terrible urge to *do* something, but what I do not know.

The music cuts off in midshriek.

"*Behold*, Brothers and Sisters!" Jimmy Divine whispers. "Witness the very *spawn* of Satan: the *Antichrists!*"

Gasps, cries, screams!

Men faint. Children hide their eyes. Teeners fight to get a better view.

"Fear not, friends," Jimmy Divine says. "They are caught like *rats* in God's trap while you and I rest *easy* in the Hands of the Lord!"

"Hallelujah!"

"Amen!"

"Have mercy!"

"Bless the Lord!"

The dark chord returns, thrumming at the edge of audibility, its ominous vibrations rippling through our flesh.

The sound seems to puff up Jimmy Divine. He looks huge on stage, a giant out of Biblical times, a consecrated man on a hallowed mission.

He whirls, points imperiously at the squad's Archangel. He bellows.

"Show!

"Us!

"God's!

"POWER!"

The Archangel pivots, and fires his rod of Aaron into a pit at the foot of the stage.

Ba-*room!*

Flames erupt.

Ba-room! Ba-room! Ba-room!

Sheets and gouts and fountains of fire flare up, spinning and twisting themselves into a hellish ball of flame.

The ball explodes. A torrent of fire spews into the sky, lances up into the night, and licks at the stars.

Screams and gasps of terror. The crowd cowers.

"From the fires of Hades did they come," Jimmy Divine thunders through the chaos, "so to the selfsame fires let them return!"

The Angels launch the air litters. The roar of the flames is deafening. Even at this distance, the heat sears.

Beside me, Angela's and Fabiola's bodies shudder. Their lips part in soundless shrieks. The flames paint their faces a hideous rippling orange.

The litters float across the stage, bearing the Children toward the fire pit.

Trembling, the crowd holds its breath.

Even if they wanted to, there is nothing anyone could do. At least this will be quick, I think, fighting to keep my eyes open against the intense heat. Not like the Crucifixion, which dragged out for hours. No taunting of the Savior to His agonized face here. No tearing of hands and feet by the weight of the body hanging from the Cross. No piercing of the side, no quenching a dying man's thirst with vinegar and gall, no casting of lots for the victim's rags, no mocking crown of thorns.

And no Last Words to echo down the ages. No *Father, forgive them, for they know not what they do.* No *My God, my God, why hast Thou forsaken me!*

I think of María de Dios, who is surely somewhere watching in horror, and recall Christ's words from the Cross to His anguished mother: *Woman, behold thy son!*

I recall His words to the good thief, Dismas, who believed in Him even to the end: *Today shalt thou be with me in Paradise.*

I recall the simple human suffering captured in these moving words: *I thirst.*

I recall His words of gratitude when the agony was at long last ending: *It is finished.*

And I recall the final words from His dying lips: *Father, into Thy hands I commend my spirit.*

I look at the Children laid out upon their litters encased in a cold living death, and find that I am weeping.

Slowly, slowly, the litters glide out over the edge of the stage. Gently, gently, they pierce the curtain of fire. Brightly, brightly, they shimmer, impervious to the raging flames.

"Milagro . . . ," someone whispers.

But no.

In the space of a breath, the tiny bodies vaporize and the litters melt, consumed like candle wax in a blast furnace.

"My God!" Fabiola whispers, her voice somehow audible to me over the shattering roar of the flames. "They've killed the Children."

"The Romans killed Jesus, too," I say, "but that didn't stop Him." The tremor in my voice robs it of conviction.

Angela begins to cry. "But He was a grown man, and they were just . . . a little boy and a little girl."

My gorge rises. I swallow with difficulty. An irresistible urge to *do* something rumbles inside me like a geyser ready to erupt.

Onstage, Jimmy Divine capers about in a frenzy. Throwing splits and backflips and cartwheels like God's own acrobat, he leads the crowd in a foot-stomping, hand-clapping chant.

"HAL-LE-LU-JAH!

"HAL-LE-LU-JAH!

"HAL-LE-LU-JAH!"

He lands on his feet, throws his arms wide like a gymnast completing a dismount, and turns his palms down for silence.

Instant hush.

Two hundred thousand eyes fix on him.

The angry voice of the fire still rules the night. Jimmy Divine's fingers splay out. His hands descend, and, like some raging serpent snaking back into its dark lair, the pyre slowly subsides.

"Brothers and Sisters!" Jimmy Divine cries into the preternatural silence. "We have *prepared* the Way of the Lord!" He skips to the right, waving his arms about. "Brothers and

Sisters! Now shall we reap our reward!" He prances to the left, leaning back and lifting his knees high like a dancer doing a cakewalk. "Brothers and Sisters! Now shall we witness the Comin' of the True Messiah!"

A chord rises from the throats of an angelic choir, heart-stoppingly lovely, sustained beyond human ability.

Light bathes the clouds.

Spotlights sweep the heavens.

Lasers slash the night.

And suddenly, high in the sky, robed in white, suspended in air, a figure appears, arms outstretched in blessing, captured in a sphere of light.

The choir crescendos. Solo voices pirouette and spiral, soar and swoop and skyrocket within the mighty chord.

Awash in glory, the figure descends.

We watch, transfixed. One hundred thousand voices cry out in amazement and ecstasy.

"I don't believe it . . . !" Fabiola whispers.

"Mother of God," Angela murmurs, "it's the Shepherdess!"

With solemn majesty, the figure alights.

The Shepherdess busses Jimmy Divine on both cheeks. "I bring you the Kiss of Peace, Brother Jimmy."

She smiles at us. She is luminous, radiant. She gleams, she shimmers.

Who would ever suspect that this vision bears on her flesh the Mark of the Beast?

The choir fades out.

"Brothers and Sisters," Jimmy Divine cries into the silence, "bear witness with me, for now it is revealed! The

Redeemer is here! The Redeemer is here! The Redeemer has been with us for, lo, these forty-four years!" Jimmy Divine is hot, Jimmy Divine is cooking. "Behold the New Messiah! Behold the True Redeemer! Behold the Second Coming of Christ!" The stage is too small to contain Brother Jimmy's fervor. The *world* is too small! "Bless us, Sister Lucy," Jimmy Divine cries, "bless us!"

The Shepherdess nods serenely. "With all my heart do I bless you, Brother Jimmy." She smiles again at the gaping throngs. "As do I bless each of you, my belovèd children!"

The crowd roars, "WE THANK YOU, DEAR MOTHER!"

The Shepherdess stands silent for a moment, face lifted to the heavens, basking in the warmth of the crowd, soaking in their vast energy. "Hear me, my children," she finally cries. "For I have come to cleanse you of your sins!"

"LORD HAVE MERCY!"

"To clasp the righteous to my bosom!"

"BLESS ME, JESUS!"

"And at long, long last to establish the Kingdom of Heaven on Earth . . . *forever!*"

"GLORY BE TO GOD!"

I am aghast. The scales have fallen from my eyes. Even without Angela's help, I finally see beneath the surface to the dark goings-on below.

The purpose of this faithless trick, this religious charade, this terrible hoax being perpetrated by my own father and the person who symbolizes all that is most holy, the purpose of this . . . this *farce* . . . is simply to consolidate their position and power.

This is meant to be the victory of Ambition, the triumph of Greed, the conquest of ultimate Power, for if tonight we accept the Shepherdess as being truly the New Messiah, how will anyone ever again place limits on her?

Who will dare say nay to God's Only Begotten Daughter?

I feel as though someone has sunk a fist in my gut, as though all the air that ever passed through my lungs has been blasted out of my body. If this travesty is allowed to succeed, then what we are witnessing, what we are joyfully welcoming and wholeheartedly celebrating, is the very horror that the Shepherdess has pretended to warn us against at every turn these past months—the dawning of the Age of the Antichrist.

This cannot be.

a v.a.s.t h.o.t r.a.g.e
l.i.k.e t.h.e b.l.a.s.t o.f m.o.u.n.t.a.i.n.s b.u.r.s.t.i.n.g
s.w.e.l.l.s i.n m.y b.r.a.i.n
a s.l.i.c.k s.h.a.r.p p.a.i.n
l.i.k.e t.h.e s.l.i.c.e o.f t.a.l.o.n.s s.i.n.k.i.n.g
b.o.i.l.s t.h.r.o.u.g.h m.y b.l.o.o.d
l.i.g.h.t.n.i.n.g s.h.a.t.t.e.r.s s.h.a.d.o.w.s
a.n.d e.r.u.p.t.s i.n.s.i.d.e m.y s.o.u.l
a w.i.l.d h.o.t v.o.i.c.e
h.o.w.l.s l.o.v.e
h.o.w.l.s j.o.y

h.o.w.l.s l.o.v.e
h.o.w.l.s j.o.y
h.o.w.l.s

"HOLD YOUR TONGUE, BLASPHEMER."
Silence, instant and utter.
Two hundred thousand cowed eyes seek the speaker.
The voice is mine.
"IF IT IS FIRE YOU DESIRE, THEN FIRE SHALL YOU HAVE!"
I am infused with a wondrous peace, the peace that sur-passeth understanding and is the fount of Grace and all true power.

Darkness blazes into day as the curved surface of the sun swells like the Eye of God in the quivering heavens. Though every human eye should be blinded, every fleshly body consumed, they are not. Fear and wonder, terror and amazement, dread and fascination, greet this howling inferno, this swirling ball of icy Godfire pulsing in the heavens.

It is terrible to witness.

But there is more.

Winds from beyond the stars blast the tears from our eyes, suck the air from our lungs, tear at our clothes and sanity, shriek and wail about us like lost souls summoned from perdition. Rumbles from the bowels of the earth shiver the ground beneath us, rattle our terrified bones, re-duce us to quivering meat. Firestorms the size of planets rage across the furious face of the sun, erupt into space, rain down on us in flaming torrents.

Oh, the wonder and the terror and the joy!

People fall to the ground, scramble to escape, whimper, while a star gone berserk rages in the midnight sky.

In that pandemonium, the Shepherdess barely whispers, yet somehow her words reach the multitude clearly, even through the howl of nature's holy fury.

"These truly were the Children of God."

She sinks to her knees. As do the multitude of souls who fill the great bowl shape.

I douse the terrible light in the burning sky. I quell the great winds from beyond the stars. I soothe the trembling earth.

I do this because they have understood.

The voices quiet. The sobbing subsides.

Once again it is true night.

On her knees at center stage, the Shepherdess weeps. "Forgive me," she says. "Please forgive me."

I know what must be done.

"Weep no more, Alma Lucille," I say. "All who truly repent are forgiven."

The Shepherdess looks dazed, but says, "I want to witness." Her words are clearly formed.

"It isn't necessary," I say gently.

"I want people to know the truth," she says.

I step back, nod. "Speak, then, and tell your truth."

The Shepherdess rises.

Levicams translate her flesh into digital signals to feed twenty-two billion hungry viddy screens. With the speed of light, her image girdles the globe and flashes to worlds beyond. It ricochets off geosynchronous satellites orbiting above Europe and Asia and the Indian subcontinent, connecting Australia and Oceania and the three Americas, floating in the warm skies of Africa and the frozen heavens of Antarctica. It zips the five hundred twenty-seven thousand kilometers to the lunar villes, zooms the five hundred forty million kilometers to the distant Martian colonies.

Alma Lucille Ferris takes a painful breath. She starts to speak, not in the familiar sensual tones of the Shepherdess but in a strange new voice, thin and oddly affecting.

The voice of a child.

"When I was little, we lived on a farm near St. Peter, Illinois," she says, into the glare of a dozen spotlights. "I was a good girl, then, and we were happy, Daddy and Mommy and me. When Mommy kissed me good-night, she always said, 'I love you, Alma Lucille. See you in the morning.' But one morning she didn't wake up, and I was only seven."

The Shepherdess is a tiny figure on a giant stage. Her naked face is magnified fifty times its normal size on half a dozen giant viddy screens scattered about the stadium, but her heart is not here. It is back then, in another time, another place.

"Wake up, Mommy," the Shepherdess pleads before a hundred thousand rapt faces. "Why don't she wake up, Daddy?" Her eyes fill with tears. They glisten in the harsh lights. "I missed her so much. Daddy said he missed her, too."

The Shepherdess pauses, momentarily at a loss, searching for something, something for which there are no child words.

"Daddy said now that Mommy'd left us, I would have to be the Mommy." She speaks slowly, the words stumbling. Fear contorts her face. "No, don't, Daddy, please! I don't want to!" She begins to sob. "No, Daddy, please, no!"

She stops, tries to catch her breath, shudders. "Afterwards he'd look at me with those angry black eyes like I'd done something terrible. And he'd whip me."

The Shepherdess stops again, panting. "Daddy was a God-fearing man," she says. Her voice drops to a whisper. "He said I was the Devil's daughter." She wipes her eyes. "Said I was the Devil's daughter sent to drag him down to perdition." Her eyes well up again. "And he called me a whore." A stricken look. "I was so scared."

The Shepherdess cuddles an imaginary doll. "Just you and me, Miz Rags," she coos. "We're all alone, you and me. Got to stick together." She kisses air, tenderly strokes imaginary curls. "I love you, Miz Rags. See you in the morning."

The Shepherdess lowers her head. When she looks up again, her voice has deepened, grown older. "When I got my period, Daddy took me to Moline, to see a tattoo man. The man's hair was greasy, and there were gaps in his teeth, and his mouth smelled like rotting eggs."

She whimpers. "The man strapped me down so I couldn't move. I called out to my Daddy for help, but Daddy just smacked me!" Tears roll down the Shepherdess's cheeks. "And the tattoo man took his needle—he had my arms pulled up over my head so I couldn't move—and he pricked numbers into my skin, the three sixes, he pricked the three sixes into the skin underneath my arm."

The faithful are aghast.

"Then Daddy had a change of heart, and tried to save me," the Shepherdess says bitterly, in the voice of a woman now. "He dragged me all over the country, to churches and revivals and tent meetings in St. Paul and Sacramento and St. Augustine and Corpus Christi. He even paid the preachers cash money to cast out the demon that he claimed had possessed me—and let me tell you, my Daddy was a tight-fisted son of a gun."

The Shepherdess laughs, something between a snort and a bark. The harsh sound is startling. "None of the exorcisms worked, though. None of the healers helped." The Shepherdess hugs her elbows, rocks in place. "So Daddy cursed me, swore at me, yelled in a terrible voice: 'You ain't cured, you little whore, 'cause you don't wanna be!'"

The Shepherdess breathes heavily through her nose. Her hand rises to her throat. "He got so angry that he grabbed me around the neck, started choking me." Her breasts rise and fall agitatedly. "I couldn't breathe. I couldn't breathe." The Shepherdess's eyes widen at some vision only she can see. "His face was right in front of mine, his features bunched up like a fist, and I looked into his eyes, sure he'd kill me this time, and I saw . . . that it wasn't me."

The Shepherdess sets her jaw, straightens. "It wasn't me. Daddy was the one possessed. Tormented by his own terrible demons." She sighs, a ragged hiss that scrapes our nerves like sandpaper. She shakes her head sadly.

"The churchfolk, they tried to turn me into a good Christian girl. 'Study your Scriptures, Alma Lucille.' 'Cover your shame, honey.' 'Gonna burn if you don't choose for Jesus, sweetheart.' Because I didn't want them to hate me, I let them have my soul."

Her face clouds. "They praised me, but they didn't love me. Not the real Alma Lucille. Not like Mommy." The Shepherdess's voice grows tender, wistful, sweet. "See you in the morning," she singsongs.

The smile fades. "They only loved the thing I pretended to be, the thing they wanted me to be. And that hurt so bad, I let a real demon possess me, a demon called Revenge."

The Shepherdess looks out at the audience inquiringly. "Maybe some of you know him?" Here and there, heads nod. "Revenge is a terrible master. Rots your insides and leaves you like a whited sepulcher on the outside. That's what he did to me."

Her eyes narrow, and her face hardens. "No, *I* did that to me. There's no laying the blame elsewhere." She closes her eyes, opens them again, speaks flatly now. "I decided to become what they wanted, and use their teachings against them." Self-contempt creeps into her voice. "And that's what brought me to where I am today: a living lie, the adopted daughter of the Father of Lies."

Many of the faithful weep openly. There is a hot, salty taste in my own mouth.

"I have sinned against you, Brothers and Sisters," the Shepherdess says, "and I have sinned grievously against Our Lord. I pray that His precious blood may cleanse my soul, for I repent most heartily for having offended you whom I called my children and Him whom I call my Father."

She sinks to her knees.

"And so I beg"—she fights to speak through her sobs— "your forgiveness."

A great silence settles over us, broken only by the sorrow of this woman.

"Rise, Alma Lucille," I say. "Your sins are forgiven." I smile encouragingly. "Rise and tell the world the message the Children brought."

The Shepherdess looks lost. "But I don't know the message they—"

Her face floods with understanding. Her shuddering stops. She smiles, a smile beyond happiness. "Of course, I know it," she says, marveling. "I've always known it."

She turns to the cameras, her face suffused with inner peace. "Brothers and Sisters," she says, her voice growing in strength and sweetness with each word, "the message is simple. It's something we have all known in our hearts since . . . always."

Her eyes are rimmed with red, swollen from weeping. Yet never has she looked more beautiful.

"It's something we've repeated so often, that most of us have forgotten its meaning."

She spreads her arms as though to embrace every soul here.

"Love one another."

She smiles sadly. "Such a simple thing, but maybe the hardest thing in the world to do." Tears brim her eyes. "Be kind to each other," she whispers. "Be gentle. Be forgiving."

We smile at each other, she and I.

"Love one another," the Shepherdess says.

"Love one another," I say.

"LO-OVE ONE AN-OTH-ER," Jimmy Divine sing-songs.

My flesh turns cold. All this time I had believed my father was a pawn in the Shepherdess's tainted hands. Now I know better.

In a rage, I turn on Jimmy Divine.

"And as for you, Great Father of Lies," I cry. *"Show your true self, Satan!"*

Spotlights pin the preacher in their pitiless glare. Cameras lock on his body and face. He becomes multitudes as his image multiplies to fill every viddy screen.

A terrifying change has overtaken him. He stands twenty meters tall. His face is lean and bony, his eyes scarlet, his fingernails long and curved, his voice an inhuman bass mixed with the whir of the rattlesnake and the rumble of the cougar.

He crouches down toward us.

"So!" Jimmy Divine sneers. "Your side wins again, soul-saver, but by the narrowest of margins. This time my victory was, oh, so close. But! I know you humans." He looks at me disdainfully. "You are weak and stupid and have pitifully short memories. You will forget this precious 'message.' And sooner than you think. You always have." His eyes glow with a ruby fire. His voice grows loud, arrogance made audible. "And next time, rest assured, I will not lose, for I am the Prince of Darkness, the Lord of the Flies, and the God of Hellfire, and I will never, *ever* serve men or their heavenly Father!"

The wrath of God boils up in my throat and these words erupt:

"IN THE NAME OF OUR FATHER, AROINT THEE, SATAN!"

With a diabolical laugh, Jimmy Divine lifts both arms sharply—an insane conductor demanding an impossible crescendo—and is consumed by lightning and devoured by thunder.

All that remains onstage is the echo of the Devil's chilling laughter.

49

Nu-meat sizzles over hot coals. It may lack Don Efraín's miraculous sauce, but it still smells delicious. Hunger pangs claw my empty stomach. María de Dios turns the shish kebab to keep it from charring. I like my meat burnt on the outside and raw on the inside. But food is not the reason I am here.

Six days have passed since Jimmy Divine's End of the World show and, in some ways, the world we knew did end. For the moment, at least, it is a different place. You see a stunned look in everyone's eyes. By now, anyone who was not watching the live satcast has seen the replay. Stations worldwide have been rerunning it at least once a day. Some doubters have tried to claim it was all a sham, a trick, an illusion, a construct of special effects, a feat of digital legerdemain. But those who saw know the truth. Violent crimes have plummeted to near nothing, church attendance has ballooned, the civil war in Mexico has shifted into peaceful negotiations, and, at the San Diego Zoo, a lion lay down with a lamb.

I would like to think it will last, but Jimmy Divine is right. Our memories are short. With time, we will forget.

"Will there be another Messiah?" I blurt out.

"Of course," María de Dios says.

I am amazed. For me, it is an enormous struggle even to shape the words, and yet María de Dios pops out the answer, just like that.

"When?" I say. "In another two thousand years?"

"When we need one most." She looks amused. "It has nothing to do with years."

"Then we won't destroy ourselves first?"

"That is entirely up to us. That is why Our Father gave us free will."

"We don't always use it wisely."

"No ... but maybe we are learning."

Her words provide me some comfort. But on this Day of the Epiphany of the Year of Our Lord 2100, I have come to see María de Dios because something else has been preying on my mind. I believe she is the only one who can set my heart at rest.

"What troubles you, Juan Bautista?"

"The Children," I say, though that is not the real issue. "I haven't said how sorry I am for your loss."

Her face clouds. She nods, remembering. "It was agony

to witness what was done to my little ones," she whispers, "a pain such as no one should have to endure." She sighs, looks at me almost shyly. "But at least they returned to me." A smile rolls the clouds away.

"They're alive?"

My voice must have sounded incredulous, because she says, "Do you find that odd?" She looks at me like a teacher wondering what to do with a slow pupil. "You know who they are."

I feel ashamed and excited at the same time. "Are they here? Can I see them?"

María de Dios turns the shish kebab. The nu-meat smells wonderfully of olive oil, cilantro, oregano, and garlic, but my hunger is forgotten.

"They are sleeping," she says. "It has not been easy for them. But I know they would want to see you. I will wake them."

Noel and Emma trundle in from the adjoining room. They smile sleepily and embrace me.

"How long have you been here?" I ask in wonder.

"Not long," Emma says. "A few days."

Noel grins. "You put on quite a show New Year's Eve."

I feel the fear harden in my belly like a stone. "That's what's been troubling me," I mumble. I look for some way to ease into this, but come up empty. "If Jimmy Divine was really the Devil, and he was my father," I say, "then what does that make me?"

The Son of Satan, I answer myself.

Noel studies me. "It makes you human, Juan Bautista, like everyone else in the world, even Emma and me."

"But . . . but you are also God."

"But we became human. We know hunger, like you; and fear, like you; and the same joys and sorrows and temptations."

"If you prick us," Emma says, "do we not bleed? If you tickle us, do we not laugh? If you poison us, do we not die?"

I do not recall that particular passage from the Bible. "But death has no power over you," I say.

"Nor over anyone. Do you still have doubts?"

I nod, unable to put my great dread into words.

"You believe you are the Son of Satan," Noel says. "You think you may be the Antichrist." It is not a question.

I nod again.

He looks at me like a patient teacher, his face the image of his mother's. "Why do you think we chose you, Juan?" he says softly. "Out of all humankind, why you?"

I shake my head.

"Because if even the child of Lucifer can be saved, then men must know there is hope for all."

"*Am* I saved?"

"That is in your hands."

Emma smiles. "You think that the sins of the father are visited upon the child. That's not true. You are free to make of yourself what you will, free to be whatsoever you choose."

"Master of my fate, huh?" I say.

Noel nods. "You always were."

"What about the . . . miracles?" I ask. "They don't exactly make me feel human."

"Humans perform miracles all the time, Juan Bautista."

"Yes," Emma says. "The mother who finds the strength to lift an overturned car to free her trapped child."

"The physician who finds a cure when there is no hope," Noel says.

"The miracle of birth."

"The miracle of death."

"The miracle of love."

"Those are different," I say, but in my heart I am starting to get the point. "I resurrected Fabiola. I vanquished Beelzebub."

Emma grins. "You're right, Juan Bautista, on those you may have had a little help."

"But the power to do all these things comes from the same Source," Noel says. "It is there for everyone when it is needed."

"Despite everything," Emma says, "you're still a normal human being, Juan, with all a normal person's doubts and worries."

"Just a regular guy, with no special powers?"

"No special powers," Emma says. "You can't fly, and," she adds with a chuckle, "I doubt you could walk on water."

"But like you said," Noel adds, "master of your own fate."

In the courtyard outside, Cristóbal plucks the strings of his cuatro.

Well, I'm glad that I love Jesus,
For He loves us one and all,
Loves my Sisters, loves my Brothers,
Loves all creatures, great and small
And I'm glad we'll be together
Come that final trumpet call,
When the sun consumes the heavens
And the stars begin to fall.

Noel punches me encouragingly on the shoulder. Takes me completely by surprise. After a moment, though, I smile and punch him back.

Makes me feel what I used to call Howie Happy.

5Ø

That night I dream.

In the dream, my soul slides out of my sleeping body and slips out the window like a wisp of steam, leaving behind Angela, lying on her side, the heart of our child beating inside her sleeping belly. A ghostly cloud, I ride the night air above my city of a billion lights.

As I waft along, I slowly realize that I have been summoned.

But by whom?

Buildings and roads give way to the blasted earth of El Vertedero where fires that were born a century ago still rage. I descend. Though bodiless, I am overwhelmed by the stench of rot and decay, of ancient refuse and viscous offal.

Flies fill the air with ceaseless buzzing. Smoke stings the eyes and burns the throat. Heat sears my skin and distorts my vision.

I have been summoned to Hell.

"Hell ain't as nice as this," says Jimmy Divine. "And this sure ain't the place I'da picked to meet you. I got a better sense of PR than that."

Jimmy Divine stands behind me, wearing a white Stetson hat and a grin as warm as a day in June.

"I'm disappointed in you, boy," he says. "You let yourself get suckered by the Other Side. I expected a little more loyalty from my own son."

All the old feelings come roiling up inside me. My resentment at his rejection, my hunger for his approval, my need to prove my own worth to him.

"I never meant anything to you," I say. "Except as a tool."

"Give me a lever long enough and I'll move the world," he says, grinning.

I get the impression he thinks he has said something clever, but I do not get it.

"What do you want from me?" I ask.

"I don't *want* anything from you. I *got* something for you."

"What are you going to tempt me with? Power? Wealth? Sex?"

"Nope. Love."

I laugh in his face. But his smile remains warm.

"You?" I say. "Love?"

"Kinda hard to swallow, ain't it? Especially comin' from the Father of Lies hisself. But it's true. You and me are more alike than you might suspect, boy. My Father turned His back on me, too. Set me a bad example for parentin', dontcha think?"

"You rebelled against Him. You refused to do His bidding."

"Got a kinda familiar ring to it, don't it?"

"It's not the same with us."

"Ain't it?"

"No. He created you."

"Like I did you?"

"No!"

"Not only are you the issue of my fleshly loins, but I shaped you in your mother's womb. Toyed with your DNA, rearranged your double helix. Ever wonder why you never get sick? Or why, in a world that's headed for Hell in a handbasket, you've enjoyed such a privileged life?"

"You?"

He bows, taps the brim of his Stetson with two fingers. "I love you, boy," he whispers. "I love you."

They are only words, but they hit hard. I have been waiting all my life to hear them from him. I had come to believe it would no longer make a difference.

But it does. It does.

"I wanna make it up to you, boy. The lost years. We've got all eternity ahead of us. Give me another chance."

The call of flesh to flesh, of blood to blood, of spirit to spirit, is more powerful than I could have imagined. My distrust and anger, my resentment and pain, are melting, running, slipping away. I long to say I am sorry, say I forgive him, call him father.

More than anything, I want his love.

"Will you give me another chance, son?"

My lips start to form the word "Yes."

"Give me the chance my Father never gave me."

The word dies in my throat. An icy lump clumps in my gut.

The chance your Father never gave you?

"You just don't know when to quit, do you, Brother Jimmy?"

This is the biggest lie of all from the tongue of the Master of Lies. I am swamped by a terrible sense of loss.

A fog has burned away, and at long last the world presents itself so clearly that even slow, dumb, pathetic Juan Bautista Lorca cannot help but see it plain, cannot help but finally take notice of the great house of untruths and deceptions his father has built around him.

Every hurt he ever inflicted on me—the rejections, the loneliness, the lack of love, all of it—explodes in my brain. The mansion comes crashing down.

"Whaddaya mean, boy?" A smile curls his lips, but it is forced, rigid. "What's your answer?"

No, I want to say. But the word is too small. Then the perfect words come to my lips:

"No, father, I will not serve you."

The smile on the Devil's face dies. A thunderclap such as might have marked the birth of the universe rattles the world. Jimmy Divine is transformed into a figure of ashes.

But his lips still move. "You think you've won, boy?" His eyes still incandesce. "Well, think again." His voice still shivers the spine. "Your son! Your son . . . is *mine!*"

Torrential rain. The figure of ashes melts and runs and sluices away.

Raindrops roll down my face.

A bolt of lightning blinds me, followed by another shattering thunderclap.

I sit up in bed, heart pounding, thunder echoing in my ears.

Angela wakes up, startled. "What is it, Juan?" She pushes a lock of hair off her forehead, rubs the sleep from her eyes. "Was it a dream?"

I nod.

"A bad one?"

I nod again. "But it didn't feel like a dream," I say. "It felt real."

The thunder has faded, and the sky outside glows with the light of false dawn, but Jimmy Divine's final words still echo in my brain.

Angela puts her hands on me. "You look so sad. And scared. What's wrong?"

Suddenly, tears. I sob. Where did this outburst come from? What is this heaviness that crushes my heart?

I weep brokenly, blubbering and hiccuping as though someone has died, but what do I mourn? The loss of a father I never had, of the innocence I did not appreciate when it was mine, of my trust in the one person I thought above suspicion?

Angela's arms enfold me, warm and comforting. I long to press against her, to mingle my breath with hers, to bury myself inside her, but my body is too stiff. I brace a hand against her belly, feel a kick.

My mind has rooted out new meaning in Jimmy Divine's parting shot, and now doubt congeals my soul: Is this child my son or is he my half-brother?

That should be simple enough to settle. Angela and I vowed never to lie to each other, while Jimmy Divine has proved himself to be nothing less than the Father of Lies.

I love Angela. I have to trust her.

She coaxes me deeper into her embrace. I succumb.

But Brother Jimmy is as insidious as a serpent. Was it just muck he showed me beneath the surface of things, or was it a terrible truth?

Outside, the sun boils up over the horizon.

ACKN⊕WLEDGⅢENTS

My gratitude and appreciation to the following people:

- for their individual contributions to the evolution of this book: Tita Stevens, James Morrow, Ashley Grayson, Miquel Barceló, Rafael Marín, the BEM boys (Ricard de la Casa, Pedro Jorge Romero, José Luis González, and especially Joan Manel Ortiz), Shawna McCarthy, Leith Adams, Morris Schorr, Lois Van Epps, and Steve Vinovich
- for his invaluable insights and suggestions for improvements: my editor, Michael Kandel